I0597542

PACIFIC FORCE

PACIFIC FORCE
BOOK 1

BLAZE WARD

Pacific Force
Pacific Force, Book 1
Blaze Ward
Copyright © 2023 Blaze Ward
All rights reserved
Published by Knotted Road Press
www.KnottedRoadPress.com

ISBN: 978-1-64470-335-9

Cover art:
ID 31906935 © Welcomia | Dreamstime.com

Cover and interior design copyright © 2023 Knotted Road Press

Reviews
It's true. Reviews help. Even a short one, such as, "Loved it!" So please consider reviewing this book (and all of the ones you've read) on your favorite retailer site.

Never miss a release!
If you'd like to be notified of new releases, sign up for my newsletter.

http://www.blazeward.com/newsletter/

Buy More!
Did you know that you can buy directly from the Knotted Road Press website?

https://www.knottedroadpress.com/shop/

This book is licensed for your personal enjoyment only. All rights reserved. This is a work of fiction. All characters and events portrayed in this book are fictional, and any resemblance to real people or incidents is purely coincidental. This book, or parts thereof, may not be reproduced in any form without permission.

ALSO BY BLAZE WARD

The Science Officer Series

Start with: The Science Officer

The Jessica Keller Chronicles

Start with: Auberon

CS-405 (Command Centurion Kosnett, part of Jessica)

Start with: Queen Anne's Revenge

First Centurion Kosnett (sequel to Jessica)

Start with: Encounter at Vilahana

Additional Alexandria Station Stories

Alexandria Station Collection

Handsome Rob (Alexandria Station Universe)

Start with: Can't Shoot Straight Gang

=====================

Corsac Fox

Start with: Flight of the Corsac Fox

Operation Marrakesh

Start with: Trial by Leviathan

Captain Daring

Start with: Revoked

The Hunter Bureau

Start with: Mirrors

Fairchild

Start with: Fairchild

Last Stand

Start with: Lost Dreams

The Lazarus Alliance

Start with: Escape

Shadow of the Dominion

Start with: Longshot Hypothesis

Star Dragon

Start with: Birth of the Star Dragon

Kincaide's War

Start with: The Eden Package

Star Tribes

Start with: Winterstar

ACTION-ADVENTURE

Pacific Force

Start with: Pacific Force

The Red Branch

Start with: Night Strike

Swordmistress Zhen

Start with: Traveler From The West

FANTASTICAL

The Gunderson Case Files, Volume 1

Augustus Derlyth, Occult Detective

Start with: Ill Tidings

CHAPTER
ONE

JAKE SURVEYED the crime scene with a grim smile on his face, leaning his weight a little on the fender of somebody's brand new 2018 Mustang in Arrest-Me-Red. Not even a GT, just a little pussy six cylinder with an after-factory, amateur-hour paint job.

He was standing back behind the strip of tape marked 'POLICE' in bright yellow, with a few other folks who were watching as the party slowly concluded with all the bad guys being marched out in cuffs. The rest of the folks around him were just innocents—drawn by sirens, fire trucks, news vans, and apparently every cop and federal agent in Seattle and the surrounding jurisdictions—to see the number of different logos and officers involved.

In the middle distance, Perkins—a tall, slender almost-bald guy with a ring of brown hair—was reading a prepared statement to a handful of cameras and a bank of lights. Jake presumed that he was giving the standard report that would be shown on every local news network as well as clips across the country.

A lot of unhappy people would see one of their principal warehouses in the background, with federal agents loading evidence boxes into unmarked panel vans to be hauled off. That made Jake happy.

Around him, Jake felt the crowd start to dissolve and head back to one of the nearby brew pubs where they'd been having a karaoke night before all this started. He shifted to the side so he could lean against an old brick wall. Deeper into the shadows, or at least harder to see.

Over there, Perkins wrapped up his bit, ignored a few questions, and walked off, seemingly at random. At least random enough that none of the reporters were paying attention as they each did their little sign-off bits and blew their night vision to hell.

There was a reason Jake was standing in semi-darkness. Not invisible, but certainly shadowed.

Perkins knew where he was. Walked right to the tape, nodded to the Seattle cop holding it up, and slipped under.

"Safe to talk here?" Perkins asked.

"Better than the bar behind me," Jake replied.

"Think we got them all," Perkins said. "Twenty arrests, so I'll have to compare faces to lists when we get them all booked, but this looks like a clean sweep. You're a dumbass for doing this by yourself though, Jake. Where's the rest of your team?"

"Pacific Force is retired, Perkins," Jake replied. "You know that. This was a one-time favor for you and your Multi-Jurisdiction Task Force. Then I'm back out of the game."

Perkins grimaced, then forced it into a grin.

"If you ever want an official job, you've got my number, Jake," he said. "The feds could use you. And the others."

"We don't want badges, Perkins," Jake replied. "We do this—excuse me—did this because a lot of the times the very people who are supposed to arrest people like that are either working for them under the table or so utterly corrupt that they can be bought frighteningly cheap. The feds aren't much better, present company excluded."

"SPD can be among the worst," Perkins agreed. "But you're tarring the rest of us with an unfairly-broad brush."

"When you start doing stop-and-frisk in rich, white neighborhoods, we'll see," Jake snapped quietly at the man. "The kids I went to high school with twenty years ago would have gotten any cop his quota for drug arrests every damned week. But they're too busy protecting the money in this town. And every other town. That goes back centuries."

At least Perkins just grunted, smart enough not to take that bait. This country was due for a reckoning on police tactics one of these days. Especially now that a smarmy television actor had gotten himself elected President, then used all his power to loot every place where his friends in Congress could protect him.

Perkins knew that, too. They'd had a few conversations, the off-the-record type where a career bureaucrat wouldn't get himself in trouble with those same political appointees.

"So, one Seattle drug and weapon smuggling ring pretty much smashed," Perkins nodded. "What do you need from me at this point?"

"My car is inside the perimeter," Jake said. "I'd like it to not be evidence so I can drive it home tonight."

"That I can manage," he replied, turning and gesturing for Jake to join him as the officer lifted the tape.

The cop had been close enough to overhear everything, but maybe was young enough to not be completely bent yet. And looked Hispanic or Native American, like maybe his family was from around Yakima or Thurston County, and he'd come to the big city for a job. Hopefully, he'd see what the white power structure was like around here and either head home to make East-of-the-Mountains better, or at least not sell his soul to the police union in this town.

They walked to where Jake's old classic had been left by the curb, hemmed in right now by the vans. Perkins offered a few rude remarks to people standing around and got one of them moved.

"You got anything lower profile?" Perkins asked as Jake cracked open the door and stood next to his favorite coupe.

It had started in a junkyard. A '39 Plymouth coupe front end welded to a 1940 Chevy coupe frame. Chopped down some, until the windshield was just barely legal. Big slicks on the back to handle the oversized Oldsmobile 454 engine that had been slipped in with Vaseline and a crowbar after it had been customized and blueprinted. Gas mileage sucked, but you needed turbo and nitrous injectors to even keep up when Jake had a straight-away to run.

The exterior had been done in a sedate electric purple that looked like a supernova on the few clear days in Seattle where you had the right sun. The interior was completely modern and largely electronic, with a full crash cage and racing harnesses, because this was not show car. It was a working beast with an armor rating sufficient to stop most small arms at short range.

Necessary in this business, where he'd had to have a few bullet impacts buffed out over the years.

"This *is* low profile, Perkins," Jake said. "Loud would be me pulling in a McLaren supercar or something equally overpowered and stupid, like so many of the people I helped you arrest. Tonight, it was necessary to get their attention. Worked, too."

"That it did," Perkins agreed as Jake pulled the door the rest of the way open and slid in.

It purred when he turned the engine over, but that was on purpose. Never let the fools know how much power they were facing if they wanted to race from a red light. Fart cans were for kids.

Jake slipped it into gear, dropped his thumbs onto the Toyota shifter buttons that had come off an old MR2 like the one in his garage, and waved at the Fed as he pulled away.

Not quite midnight, but Jake knew he was way more wound up than he'd been willing to let Perkins see. He crossed up to I-5 and headed north, dropping onto 520 to cross the new floating bridge. Traffic on a Thursday was a little heavier than normal, but Jake needed a drive to relax. No music, just the hum of the tires and the roar of the engine.

Still, he picked them up as they started to close. Something about the way they were driving didn't smell right. Big SUV, like a Suburban or an Expedition. Way too many lights across the front, all of them on and probably blinding everyone else, but Jake's glass had been tinted and treated with various things to mute that crap when idiots drove with their high beams on. Way too common in this town.

Closing. Weaving in and out dangerously, like they were trying to catch up to *someone*. Traffic was flowing about sixty across the bridge right now. Sedate, for Seattle drivers.

The SUV was closing at about eighty. A vehicle that big got unstable at those speeds.

Jake kept one eye on the ragged zipper of cars in front of him and left most of his attention on the SUV. The weather was dry tonight, so his suspension was gripping down hard, to the point he could feel every grain of sand on the road. Yet the ride was so smooth it still felt like silk.

He had wondered earlier if maybe somebody had gotten away tonight after all. Or been late to the party and then watched from across the street until they had identified Jake and decided to follow him. He had a pistol on his hip, mostly for show, but he could have used it. Plus, he'd had half the feds in King County within sight back at the arrest.

Someone apparently wanted a private party.

Jake saw an arm come out of the passenger front window as the SUV started to come along side. Looked like it had a pistol or a submachine gun in it. He pedal-shifted down two gears, slammed his foot to the floor, and took a really good grip on the steering wheel.

He owned a third generation Toyota MR2 Spyder, back in the garage, custom rebuilt for street racing. He drove that around when he wanted something a little less flamboyant than an electric purple classic. He'd bought it secondhand from an old gearhead who'd had to retire and sell everything after a nearly fatal stroke. It was a mid-engine design, and Jake liked those, but that took practice to handle, with all the weight behind you.

He still preferred a huge hunk of angry steel in front of him and a drive shaft howling as the surge of gasoline got turned into raw acceleration.

Gunshots, but behind him. Back where he'd been before he made the jump to warp speed. The Plymouth was at eighty and rising, throwing a little smoke on the tires even at this speed.

The SUV took a few moments to catch on. And then to accelerate. Picked a bad place to do it, too, as they both were climbing up that big hill to Bellevue right now. Didn't lose them, though. Just got a nice head start.

Less chance they would be firing randomly at innocent cars. Jake doubted that he'd be lucky enough to blow by a cop or state trooper right now. He did smile at his favorite burger drive-in as he roared past it. Seattle was always a Dick's Burgers kind of town, but Jake preferred Burgermaster every time.

Up the hill now, curving around to his right. The SUV was keeping up, but only because Jake backed everything down some. Tantalize them with those taillights. Draw them in. The Plymouth could top out at a speed where the SUV wouldn't ever catch him if he really wanted them to.

The SUV got crappy gas mileage, but the Plymouth was probably worse and had a smaller tank, so he couldn't just run them dry. Especially not doing shit like this.

So he let them stay close. Over that long curving left-hand on-ramp to 405. Luckily, nobody was headed west and needing to merge.

Eighty miles per hour now. Ninety as they hit the straight and climbed. One hundred as they wove in and out of the thin, night-time traffic.

The SUV was rocking now, but Jake figured they'd gone all-in on one of those lift kits to make it ride a little higher when a vehicle like that was already top-heavy.

Good enough.

He cut suddenly from the left, all the way across the freeway to hit the off-ramp to NE 85th, wondering if they'd be able to make that drift without losing it.

Came close, from the way the ass-end slewed around a little, but the roads were apparently dry enough to hold, so he had them on his ass again.

Now, the fun part.

Not many cars he'd be willing to try this with. Certainly not at these speeds. He owned two, though.

Jake downshifted hard and more or less drifted too fast into the off-ramp headed west down the hill to Kirkland and the lake. The SUV was having a hell of a time keeping up, but the driver gunned it now to try to catch him as he got onto surface streets.

Bad choice, though. Jake hit the bottom of the off-ramp and was lucky enough that nobody wanted to merge into his lane as he blew right under the bridge and downshifted enough to make the engine howl with fury. If they had a window open, they'd hear that and maybe overreact. He stayed in the right lane right back up onto the other ramp.

The westbound 85th to southbound 405 cloverleaf onramp was the tightest, nastiest one Jake was aware of around here. You were supposed to take it at a sedate, controlled speed, getting out onto the top at thirty-five and using the straightaway up there to accelerate for merging.

Jake put the pedal to the floor and listened to the engine scream as the rubber grabbed hold.

He loved this circle. This and his MR2 were the only cars he knew that could do this without squealing the tires. He was doing seventy halfway up the curve. Behind him, the SUV driver realized that Jake was getting away and floored it.

Then the guy tried to take that curve.

Jake watched those headlights tilt and roll over suddenly as the driver lost control, slewed into the steel barrier on his left, and was too top-heavy for the thing to stop him from tumbling right over the edge of it. At least there were trees there to stop them from rolling in front of any oncoming cars.

He lifted his foot off the gas now and let the Plymouth slow down to sane speeds on this road as he watched the SUV tumble to a stop behind him.

He pulled his phone out of his pocket and pushed the voice-command button.

"Call Perkins," he said simply, watching traffic, but nobody was chasing him.

"What's up, Jake?" The fed was on the line almost instantly.

"Redmond," Jake replied. "Onramp to southbound 405. Somebody was shooting at me across the bridge, lost control, and tumbled his SUV pretty hard. You might want to come over and see if it's anybody else you want to arrest."

"You stopping to check?"

"Not a chance," Jake laughed. "One and done. And only for you."

He hung up and chuckled, driving like a proper civilian now, rather than a maniac. Everyone drove more or less politely as he considered what restaurants might be open for a quick bite. He'd need some downtime and carbs if he was going to sleep at all tonight, especially after that spike of excitement.

His phone chirped and Jake picked it up to check, glancing down.

Email from Spencer that simply read: CALL ME!!!

Three exclamation points meant serious, so Jake hit his speed dial.

"What's up?" he asked when the man answered instantly.

"We've got trouble."

CHAPTER
TWO

JAKE STOOD off to one side and watched the afternoon class work slowly through a set of martial arts forms. He wasn't personally familiar with the art they were practicing, but he'd only studied karate in his time, and this was a variant of kung fu he'd never pursued. In the end, there were only so many ways to move, step, and strike, though. The only question was what order they were assembled in.

He'd slept some last night after talking to Spencer. Had breakfast. Made it here fairly early in the morning. He could sleep another time.

The teacher had noted him as he approached across the open space of the park, but she had pointedly ignored him other than that, focusing on her half-dozen students, all older women dressed in matching black pants and tunics. Jake watched.

He did smile at the age discrepancy, as the woman teaching looked to be half the age of the youngest student, with a couple that might have been in their seventies. But they were all moving slowly and with graceful surety as hands came up and they turned in unison. It wasn't tai chi chuan, at least not the classical form he'd studied at one point, but it seemed to be a variant designed to help keep older women limber.

They finished up as he leaned against a tree that was just starting to get serious about leafing out. Seattle had been a little slow getting warm this spring, so the flowers were only now coming up. A nice breeze blew through the section of the park's parking lot that was dry enough, since it had only misted a little overnight and then blown on.

Jake didn't know if the group would have met in the rain. The woman teaching probably would have been out here practicing in anything less than real rain, but she was something of a hardass about things like that.

Finally, they were alone, the two of them. A couple of the older women had politely inquired about the stranger but smiled at whatever they'd been told then went on their ways.

Jake wondered if she'd told them he was an old boyfriend. Technically true, however long ago that had been.

He stayed against the tree and let Hollyanne walk towards him. That way, Jake wasn't invading her space.

Closer, she was still the same woman she'd been when he first met her at thirteen. Older by twenty-five years, sure. He suspected that her long, black hair wasn't naturally that color anymore, but it wasn't his place to say anything to her. It looked good against her dark, Persian skin.

Chiseled cheekbones. Perfectly manicured eyebrows that made her face seem even more warm and lively. Maybe the nose was a little long for the inverted triangle of her face, but she was still beautiful.

Five foot one. Slender, only in the way that barbed wire was slender. Hard. Deadly. Hopefully still a goof.

"Did you hear the news?" Jake asked as she stopped about six feet away.

She nodded just enough to call it a thing.

"Spencer sent me an email to let me know," Hollyanne replied in a quiet, calm voice.

It was Jake's turn to nod.

Spencer was the nerd. The journalist forever tracking down information, data, stories, hints, and rumors. He had probably emailed everyone else about the time he texted Jake last night. But that would be right.

They watched each other for a long moment.

"Why are you here, Jake?" Hollyanne asked finally, probably realizing that she couldn't wait him out.

"I dunno," Jake replied with a fake shrug. "I figured that Nathaniel Hoestler breaking out of an English prison might be important enough to do something about."

"You don't think the police can do anything?" Hollyanne retorted.

"They couldn't before," Jake reminded her. "Has anything changed?"

"We're two years older," she replied. "The Team has been retired that long. Unless you're here to tell me we have to get it back together."

"We don't have to do anything, Hollyanne," Jake said. "But I don't think that anyone else can stop him. Plus, being locked in a stone box for two years isn't likely to have made Nathaniel rethink his life. Pretty sure he's still pissed at all of us for putting him there. And everything else going back twenty years. If nothing else, he's likely to come after at least one of us."

"You, or me?" she asked with a faint grin.

He shrugged, for real this time.

"Nathaniel has his reasons to hate us both," he reminded her.

It was her turn to shrug.

"It won't ever be over, will it?" she finally asked in a voice that was too tired for the day.

"I thought it was over when we finally caught him and put him in jail," Jake said. "But we forgot about his people. I'm guessing we'll need to take them all down as well this time."

"I won't kill," Hollyanne said bluntly.

"Not asking you to, Hollyanne." Jake let a little fire build now. "You are probably the best suited to control the damage if it comes to that. To not kill, in that eyeblink. But the rest of the world wasn't enough to stop Nathaniel before. He knows too many people and has corrupted too many officials for anyone to move against him. That was why we had to get involved."

"We're private citizens, Jake McNeil," she said tartly.

"Which means corrupt cops and governments don't like us any more than criminals do, Hollyanne Kadjar," he replied. "Last time, he nearly blew up London before we stopped him. I don't know about you, but I don't want to be sitting in my big mansion and wake up one morning to the news that he's blown up something else because somebody thought his threats were idle and empty. Do you?"

Jake took a deep breath when he finished, aware that his voice had gotten a little loud. Hollyanne watched him for a long second and then a smile appeared on her face.

"Who would have imagined that a little computer club would have made such a huge difference to the future of the world?" she asked.

"Made us all rich," Jake pointed out. "How many people do you know could retire at seventeen and never have to work? Set us up to make a difference."

She nodded now, her shoulders pulled in a little and hunched against a nonexistent breeze.

"Too bad Nathaniel didn't stay with us," she said quietly.

"It would have never been big enough for him." Jake nodded as well.

"But he might have chosen a different path, Jake," Hollyanne offered. "He might not have chosen to become such a villain."

Jake shook his head ruefully.

"No, that was always in the cards for Nathaniel."

NATHANIEL STOOD FACING a big picture window with a magnificent view of East London and the Thames, hands clenched angrily behind his back.

The day had dawned wet. Not a misty drizzle like he grew up with in Seattle, but that nasty, pissing mess that soaked you in the distance from the curb to the door and threatened to drown you in the time it might take to walk to a pub.

And umbrellas wouldn't work in this wind. You'd just end up Mary Poppins-ing yourself right off the ground when a gust hit, then you'd either land in the river somewhere, or maybe the front parking lot of Scotland Yard if the gods were feeling particularly malevolent.

He checked his tie in the reflection as he ignored the three men waiting patiently behind him. Bright blue and white stripes, reflecting his first love: Brighton & Hove Albion F.C. Expensive silk. He'd gotten it on that one trip to Macao. Nathaniel smiled at that memory. Better times.

Before.

Severely blue suit. Single-breasted with three buttons

and pinstripes cut with a razor and painted with a hand better suited to sumi-e.

His hair was growing back out. In prison, he'd kept it exceptionally short, just because you never got all the bugs and things unless you fully shaved it. He'd washed religiously instead. Now, he had a stylish faux hawk that that made his long, rectangular face and square jaw almost look aquiline.

Someone had actually told him that with his shallow, sharp cheekbones he looked like that one American sports reporter. On the one hand that was good, because it would distract. On the other, Peelers looking for him might suggest a name to jog a memory, and they would light up for having seen him.

Give him another two months and it would be back to shaggy.

But Nathaniel didn't have two months. Someone had screwed up.

It was a minor thing. It might have even been glossed over in the larger milieu of his prison break, but someone had posted a recruiting call for members of his old gang on one of the Brighton & Hove Albion F.C. web boards where the more hooligan set frequently hung out.

All well and good, but he hadn't approved it. Too soon. It had been taken down as soon as someone mentioned it to him, but the damage had been done. Nathaniel had to assume that Spencer or one of Jake's other people would have seen it and thus presume that Nathaniel was still in England.

Nathaniel sighed quietly, took a breath, and turned to the three men.

Tommy was standing behind the chair, but he was a short man. Big, in the way of thugs who eat and drink too much, but still five-foot-seven inches tall, nonetheless. He always reminded Nathaniel of an English bulldog that had been crossed with a rabid American badger and then beaten with a tire iron a few times to toughen him up. His hands looked like he'd put them into a running garbage disposal a few times, but that was the years of bare knuckles brawling in underground tournaments before Nathaniel had given him a better job.

Standing next to him was Sokoro, the Kenyan. *Lucky*. Bastard claimed to be Masai, but that was just height and skinniness. His father was a judge back in the home country. The son was an embarrassment sent off to England for an education that was supposed to have involved law school, instead of petty crime convictions. His brothers and sisters had all stayed straight, but there was always one runt in the family, even at six foot four.

Mikhail was seated. Nervous. Sweating a little, even, in spite of the room being a bit cool.

Nathaniel had managed to rent an office configured for a lawyer. A barrister, since he was in England and not Seattle. It had come with nice furnishings, mostly in dark wood. There were even law books on the shelves, but they had been left by the previous tenant, the one who had fled six hours ahead of an Interpol indictment on drug smuggling charges.

Nathaniel figured that they'd negotiated a reasonable discount on the space, since the landlord would have been stuck waiting for the rest of the lease to expire had he not been able to sublet like this.

And Nathaniel liked that big, heavy, imposing desk as he moved next to it. That did something for the psyche. Right now, it provided him a spot to flip a leg up and rest his hip as he stared down at Mikhail from up close.

"Normally, I like ambition and enthusiasm to figure out what needs to be done and just going after it, Mikhail," Nathaniel began.

The punk in the old jeans, black shirt, and grungy jacket started to smile, but then the words registered. But English wasn't Mikhail's first language. That would be Russian. Nathaniel had picked him up with a bunch of others when the Chechen Wars finally ended in 2009. Mercenaries for the most part, with experience in Russian and sometimes Soviet special forces.

Killers without a conscience.

Sometimes Nathaniel thought of them as a box of guns. Point. Shoot.

But occasionally they jammed.

"You fucked up, Mikhail," Nathaniel continued as the Russian mercenary's face fell. "I have to assume that my enemies know where to look for me now. We went through a lot of effort to make it look like I had escaped to Spain and then maybe Algeria. Some of those folks will start looking closer to home because of you."

"Set a trap?" Mikhail offered in a thick, brutish accent, smiling helpfully.

"Oh, we are," Nathaniel replied.

He looked up at Tommy and nodded.

The rabid badger had a sap in one hand. It connected with the back of Mikhail's head with a harsh, meaty crunch that knocked man and chair over onto the thick, lush, slate gray carpet. Tommy being Tommy, he dropped to one knee and gave the man an extra whack, just to be sure.

Tommy looked up hopefully now. Sokoro had only moved enough that Mikhail hadn't spilled blood onto his shoes. Both men smiled.

"I want his body found in South London," Nathaniel

said coldly. "Battersea would be best, but Peckham would be acceptable."

"Either, boss?" Tommy asked with a voice like an industrial meat grinder hitting some bones.

"The Russians don't care who he is, once he's dead," Nathaniel replied. "The Brits are incompetent. The Americans would say something, but the right people will know to kill any mention of his more recent activities, so they'll just assume an underworld hit and mark it case closed."

"McNeil and Kadjar?" Tommy asked in a voice filled with wonder and hope, in the same way that a starving dog whines when you put the bowl down in front of them.

"Someone will let them know," Nathaniel said. "We'll draw them in and finish them off this time."

"Right, then," Tommy slipped the sap into the pocket of his dark jacket. "Lucky, grab his feet and we'll put him in the boot of Davey's car."

Nathaniel watched the two men lift the soon-to-be-dead mercenary and carry him from the room.

Two years. Jake and the Pacific Force had cost him two years. Only the fact that he'd gotten out of all his bitcoin investments early had kept Nathaniel from being completely broke right now. Real estate was always a better choice, since the English didn't care where your money came from as long as you were quiet about things.

It was only when you pissed off the locals that they started allowing American regulators access to the bank records.

Even that would dead end, as some of the towers he owned had been bought with boxes of gold bars, but the Gulf folks preferred that to electronic transfers. Safer. Anonymous.

If he'd had a year, Nathaniel could have come up with

something truly extravagant. But Mikhail had told the Hooligan Crew to gather up in London.

That would bring Nathaniel's old friends, too.

At least he would finally get his revenge on Jake McNeil.

JAKE WAS IN HIS KITCHEN, a space so huge that it almost needed its own zip code, but the house had come like this when he'd inherited it from his parents. And, truth be told, he did entertain just frequently enough that having this much space for a catering crew to take over made everything run smoother.

But he hardly used any of it. How many people needed two dishwashers, a walk-in freezer, double-oversized-refrigerators side by side, two stoves, and two grills, one of which was scaled for a small restaurant?

Jake was seated at the long counter that separated that space from the smaller dining room, sipping some espresso. That machine and the microwave in the nearest corner were almost always sufficient.

A shadow appeared in the archway next to him. Utterly silent, but she was like that.

Rik. Technically *Erika*, but she hated that name. Kept the Rik part just piss off her parents, who had run in the same circles as Jake's had when his were still alive.

She had a bottle of pre-made, flavored coffee in one

hand, not liking his espresso habit. Starbucks brand with mocha. Cold, like she liked it.

Rik Farrell was a big woman. Five-foot-eleven. 165 pounds. Her grandmother had been Japanese, come to the States as a war bride in the '50s. In Rik, all the recessives had lined up just right.

Naturally curly hair down to her shoulder blades. A natural blond, too, eyebrows and everywhere else. Busty and curvy, with bright blue eyes. But Japanese bones in her face and eyes. Beautiful and exotic.

Like him, she'd grown up in the gated communities of the East Side, back when Seattle was just turning into a technology town. Unlike him, she'd consciously turned herself into a redneck. Well, they'd both been rebels, hers just went against everything her parents had expected when they had dressed their little towheaded blonde in pink. Today she was in grease-stained jeans and a *NIN* T-shirt.

"Spencer just beeped the gate," she said, pulling up the stool next to his and sitting down. They were almost eyeball level this way.

Jake nodded.

"Hollyanne should be here soon," he said.

Rik brightened and took a drink of her cold coffee.

"Oh?"

"She still doesn't like girls," Jake said, watching Rik deflate a little.

"Oh."

Rik preferred girls. Was open-minded enough that he and she occasionally slept together, but she was technically also his employee, so she had to ask, and didn't have that itch all that often.

"Anybody heard from Grant?" Rik asked as she took another sip.

"Toronto," Jake replied.

"How'd he score a residency permit?" Rik jolted back a little in surprise.

"Seduced someone, duh." Jake laughed. "Emotional, physical, or financial is really the only question at that point."

"Yeah, okay, I deserved that," she laughed with him.

They sat and drank coffee companionably as they waited. There was enough drizzle to be seen through the window that Mrs. Johnson would probably remain in the guest cottage all day unless there was a problem. She was deep into mixing her next album, having previously convinced him to let her convert it to a professional-grade studio.

Occasionally, some of her friends chose to stay here so they could record with her, paying rent and understanding not to trash the place. She'd never made it as a rocker, but apparently had known everybody in town in music in the early '90s, and still had some amazing big names on speed dial.

She didn't need to be part of this conversation. Jake and Nathaniel had an understanding that even at their worst, families were always off-limits. Everyone's, his included. Mrs. Johnson would be safe, regardless of what happened next.

Spencer came in the front of the house and yelled.

"Burglars," he called. "Come to steal your shit."

"Kitchen," Jake yelled back.

He was surprised when Hollyanne walked in with Spencer, still holding her motorcycle helmet with the Go-Pro mounted on the side like a parrot. Must have snuck in behind Spencer.

Everyone hugged. Jake kissed Hollyanne on the cheek, got a harrumph, so he kissed Rik as well. Spencer got pissy, so everyone got kissed, just to shut them all up.

Spencer pulled a new bottle from the nearest fridge—that nasty energy drink he lived on—but Mrs. Johnson had known he was coming. Plus, she kept a supply anyway, since the team got together socially occasionally, at least when people passed through Seattle.

Hollyanne was drinking some sort of weird, faded yellow coconut/pineapple juice mix from the smell of her travel mug.

Jake studied Spencer as they all settled. Armenian ancestry, so just about as dark as Hollyanne, but he wasn't Persian nobility like she was. Five-foot-ten. One-fifty. Skinny and wiry. Ran marathons competitively.

He and Spencer had started the little computer club when they were in seventh grade at that private school that everyone had attended. The man was still a computer nerd, able to grok an insane number of languages, though like the rest of them he didn't need a job working for anyone else. Jake had designed the game and written a lot of the base code after Nathaniel told them all to take a flying leap. Spencer had written the primitive AI that handled bad guys. Hollyanne had understood close combat and got all that right for them. Rik had redesigned all the screens to make them "less stupid and ugly." Grant, of course, had taught the machines how to interact with players in a way that might be seduction or intimidation. Even then, he'd been the expert.

"What's so funny?" Spencer spoke up now.

"Thinking back to 2000, man," Jake continued to chuckle. "Best damned timing possible, you know?"

That got a round of laughs. To sell a computer game in February 2000 for astronomical prices and take only cash instead of stock that six months later would have ended up worthless. One of the studios that sold to the biggest software company in the world, just up the road, had eventually ended up owning the IP after everything shook out, but the five of them had split forty million dollars when they were all sixteen or seventeen.

"Tell me we've done good with it," Hollyanne said with a touch of urgency.

Everyone turned her way, but she was the philosopher of the group, forever worrying about the ethics of taking all that money and forming Pacific Force as a private, mercenary venture to stop people like Nathaniel Hoestler from doing bad things. Little things, at first, like computer crime or crime facilitated by an always-on, international communications network, but their efforts had grown world-wide eventually.

However, at the same time, they'd sort of created Nathaniel as a supervillain. His own competing game had been all set to launch in the fall of 2000, but all the money had escaped from the deflating balloon of the dot bomb, leaving him broke, bitter, and vengeful.

"We stopped someone from blowing up Big Ben," Rik reminded her. "Threw his ass in jail for it. Not my fault they couldn't hold him."

"And don't forget the Vancouver Incident," Spencer added. "Plus, the time he was planning a massacre in Beijing."

"And it goes beyond Nathaniel," Jake said. "Petrograd. Rome. Lisbon. Buenos Aires."

"We've done good," Rik assured her and everyone else.

"So why are we so convinced that he'll start up again as soon as he gets out?" Hollyanne asked, eyes focused on him now.

Jake wasn't uncomfortable with that look. If he was the

mastermind of the group, she'd always been the lancer, questioning things, but willing to go right in toe-to-toe with any bad guys that came along. They'd had similar conversations so many times he'd lost count.

"It's Nathaniel," Jake said simply. "If he was going straight, he wouldn't have let them break him out. He'd have turned himself in. Instead, he went to ground, and the world won't know where he is until he strikes again or takes some most hostages and starts issuing demands."

"Uhm," Spencer said, causing every head to turn his way. He nodded and squirmed a little. "So, I got an email from a friend…"

Everyone laughed in spite of the seriousness. Spencer was connected to so many people that his phone was programmed to play different tunes depending on which level of priority a mail or call might have, instead of just who was calling.

"Yeah, yeah," he continued. "And there's a guy who is a known associate of Nathaniel…"

"Hooligan, mercenary, or something else?" Rik asked.

"One of the Russians," Spencer confirmed. "Mikhail Ivanov. Remember him?"

"I do," Hollyanne said darkly. "Leads with his left foot. Tendency to rely too much on elbow strikes. What about him?"

"They found his body in South London," Spencer replied, pulling out his phone and checking something. "Near where the old Battersea Power Station was. Coroner said he'd been beaten severely and then executed at short range with a pistol. Body dumped for the cops to discover. I think he was also the one that posted on the Brighton board about recruiting before it was taken down, but I haven't gone all the way to the bottom of their logs to confirm it."

"Someone sending a message," Rik observed.

"But to whom?" Jake asked. "There are any number of ways to make a body disappear in London. Dumping him like that smacks of publicity. One of Nathaniel's enemies?"

"Or is it aimed at us?" Hollyanne spoke up. "Who would care about a third-rate punk getting what he had coming, except that he was connected with a major terrorist and financier who just broke out of prison?"

"Oh, I assume it's a trap," Jake nodded. "For that specific reason. If they were going after Nathaniel's crew, there would have been more bodies. Or they would just vanish."

"Maybe he pissed off Nathaniel directly?" Spencer asked.

"Likely, since you said they took down that announcement almost immediately," Jake said. "Sounds like he jumped the gun and got punished for it."

"Then what do we do?" Hollyanne asked the group.

"That's why I reached out to all of you," Jake said. "Pacific Force has always been a thing that could go places where law enforcement and espionage might not because we don't have to play by the rules."

"And we don't start the conversation with drone strikes," Hollyanne noted.

"Right, we're not like the American government," Jake agreed. "Or the Brits, the French, or the Russians."

He paused to draw a breath and finish his espresso.

"I don't think anybody else can stop Nathaniel, if only because they don't see him as that big of a threat," he continued. "Not yet. And I'd rather be going after him than letting him come after us. Safer for us and the whole world."

"You think it's time to get the band back together?" Hollyanne smiled.

Jake nodded. It was a foregone conclusion.

"Pacific Force needs to come out of retirement."

CHAPTER
FIVE

HOLLYANNE FREQUENTLY HAD her doubts about many things. She'd spent too many years on a dojo floor and around martial philosophers to find surety in anything.

Rik had retired for the evening. Knowing Spencer, he'd set up his laptop in the kitchen and be following the Asian markets for a while before going to bed. That left her and Jake sitting in the upstairs library, sipping at some exquisite adult beverages.

Jake liked whiskey, but she'd never developed the taste for it neat. Instead, she had a highball glass half-filled with brandy that his parents always kept around the house when she visited.

Jake was just finishing up his phone call.

"Grant will catch a red-eye flight to London tonight and be there first thing tomorrow," he said, setting his phone face down on the table between them.

The season was late for a fire, but Jake had a small one going, mostly for look and smell rather than heat. The two of them were in comfortable chairs, facing the fireplace with a table and bottles between them.

"He going deep cover?" Hollyanne asked, turning tactical now in spite of the glass in her hand.

Or maybe because of it. Shit was about to get serious again.

Jake nodded to her.

"For now," he said. "If this is a trap, he can work into it sideways and maybe vanish in the splash we're likely to make when we get there in a few days."

Hollyanne grimaced.

"What?" Jake asked.

"If it's Nathaniel, he'll be expecting us to follow our normal pattern of doing things, right?" She stared into the brandy like it held precognitive tea leaves. "Should we do something sideways?"

"Like what?" Jake queried.

"He'll have a plan," she continued. "He always does. I want to upset it."

"Okay. How?"

"What you do isn't predictable." Hollyanne smiled to take the sting out of her words. "But *how* you do it is. I want to hit him out of left field."

"Should you take command on this one?" Jake turned to look at her now.

"No, because I'm just as emotionally compromised around him as you are, just for different reasons," she grimaced again and fell silent.

Jake watched and waited.

"Let's take a private jet right now," she said. "Tonight. Everyone's here. Refuel someplace off his radar, like Portland, Maine. Land in maybe Liverpool or Manchester and catch the train into London quietly. Have Grant be the obvious one that Nathaniel and his people will be looking for."

"Sure," Jake agreed. "Backwards from how I'd run this investigation. I like it. You want to go wake up Rik?"

"Absolutely not!" Hollyanne laughed. "She'd try to drag me into bed with her, and it would either be a fight, or we'd never get out of here on time."

"I thought you didn't like girls," Jake observed.

"Usually," Hollyanne corrected him. "Most women are too fragile or brittle. Plus, I have spent a lot of time in weird monasteries where there were no men over the last few years. You learn to make do."

"Plus, we're not twenty anymore," Jake nodded.

"And that," she agreed. "Thirty-seven used to be ancient."

"Fine." Jake stood now. "You have Spencer get us a plane and I'll roust the Valkyrie from her beauty sleep."

"Don't trip and fall." She snickered as she rose as well. "She might pin you down and have her way with you."

He shrugged and Hollyanne understood that there was more there than she'd realized. Rik had never married. Nor had Jake. Hell, only Grant had, but he'd been divorced three times now, never able to emerge from being the con artist he was born to play even when he found a good woman.

Not that Grant would know a good woman if she walked up and bit him. But still.

Still, this felt right. The Pacific Force never just rushed right in. They always took it methodically.

Nathaniel would be counting on that, so hopefully she could force him to make a mistake.

Next time, she might not just knock the man out.

CHAPTER
SIX

GRANT COLLINGWOOD. He'd gone ahead and used his own passport this time after Jake had called back with a change of tactics. The Immigration officer studied his picture and then his face, as if the two somehow didn't go together all that well.

Average. That was a term more than one person had used to describe him, but Grant preferred *Mean* in the statistical sense, which was a much more complicated thing with many more interesting meanings. He was that central point that confused people, because everywhere he went, Grant was likely to run into someone who knew a guy who looked just like him, somewhere else.

Forgettable, in that sense, then, because he would remind them of someone, but that meant that they'd lock onto a couple of details that happened to be close and forget the rest.

And maybe Grant was that other guy, just in a different guise. Dressed different. Hair different. Slouched. Lifts in his shoes. Tanned. Pale.

Chimerical, but nobody ever understood what he

meant. Drifting in and out of roles, even when he had to play himself.

Whoever the hell Grant Collingwood really was.

Right now, the Officer grunted something, and he was through and into London.

Land of the Angles. Lovely place. He stopped long enough to get his suitcase and didn't even get lost looking for the right train to take him downtown, where he was booked to stay at a charming place on a nice street literally across from the Queen's garage with discrete men carrying submachine guns against need.

Tourist season was still a ways off, so the roads would be less crowded, but that just meant it would be beastly for someone to track him and remain anonymous.

The train ride to London was a bit crowded with other folks arriving from Canada on business, so he didn't stand out in the slightest. Grant prepared for every role, even the ones he assumed on the fly while running for his life from men with guns through the back streets of Kolkata.

Still, Grant was somewhat surprised when a familiar face happened to drift up next to him walking along as they made their way along the Underground platform, like a traveler who just happened to be heading in the same direction.

Unforeseen, but not exactly a surprise. Still, Grant didn't address the man, unsure what name might be appropriate today.

"Coffee sounds good," the man said idly, turning this way like they were traveling companions.

"It does," Grant agreed.

Obviously, someone in the British government had marked his unannounced arrival and had decided to follow up in person. Thankfully, Grant wasn't trying to smuggle anything in this time that would give them an excuse to pick him up and haul him somewhere for one of *those conversations*.

In any case, he followed the man up the escalator to the surface and walked beside him into a coffee franchise similar to the ones back home, standing behind him in line and catching that the name on the side of the cup should be *Steve*.

He didn't look like a *Steve*, but who was *Grant* to argue?

They found a table away from everyone else and put down their almost-identical suitcases.

"Forecast still sunny and cool today?" Grant asked as they got their coffee and stared at each other across the battlefield of a coffee shop table.

"Last I checked," Steve answered blandly.

"That's good," Grant noted. "Have some sightseeing planned this afternoon, after a quick shower and lunch."

"That's what concerns us," Steve said, still not using Grant's name, even though it appeared to be on the tip of the man's tongue. "We'd like to be kept in the loop."

Grant smiled amiably at the man. He'd never asked what Steve did. Or rather, exactly who he did it for. Those sorts of things were just left on the table to roll off when nobody was looking, leaving a prettier picture when the after-action reports were written up.

Somewhere in that beast called *British Intelligence*, with a law enforcement background and before that military. It was there in the way the man walked. Grant thought that they were about the same age. Late thirties. Bland in that forgettable way men like them practiced constantly.

Grant had never imagined himself as a spy, but he supposed that to be the role he filled with Pacific Force.

That, and talking to men and women like this. Shame they hadn't sent *Deborah* to chat him up today.

"I'll see what I can do," Grant offered. "Do you have a card with current contact information?"

Slight emphasis on the *current* part. Probably had a dozen numbers that all routed to this one phone, and had to be evasive when it rang if your number wasn't programmed in. Might be Steve for a while. Or not.

Steve palmed a business card then shook hands as they rose.

No message had been delivered. Well, they knew who he was, and that he was here, but that was no surprise. Other tongues would wag. News would get out.

Steve departed immediately, which was fine. Grant gave him a head start as he memorized the phone number and email address. He'd pick up a local phone this afternoon to use as a burner while he was here.

Then he would start stalking London's underworld, looking for his old mate, Nathaniel Hoestler.

CHAPTER
SEVEN

JAKE APPRECIATED GETTING lucky and knowing people who had been made fantastically wealthy by the explosions of various tech companies in Seattle over the last generation. A close family friend had left his Bombardier Global 5000 behind in Seattle while he was sailing down to San Francisco with his family. One quick call and they'd gotten the aircraft and crew prepped and taken off by two in the morning, headed east in luxury.

The best part was that this beast had the range to fly them direct to Manchester without having to stop anywhere.

Spencer was finally asleep. As was Hollyanne. There was a cute stewardess up front, more or less ignoring everyone except to peek out every once in a while and see what folks might need.

He sat in a comfortable chair made of leather clouds and watched Rik work.

"How many of those comic books are you going to sign?" he asked.

She looked up and smiled.

"Pacific Force Issue Number One, with signature." She

smiled in a most evil way. "Got twenty here. Worth a lot of money on the comic convention circuit. More if you wanted to sign a few."

She held out a stack. Jake sighed and took them, flipping up the tabletop arm.

"Do you really need the money?" he asked as she handed him the small Sharpie she'd been using.

"No, but the fan service helps," Rik replied. "Doubly so if we're back in business. There are people out there who make money from what we do."

"This is a one-time thing," Jake glowered at her.

"Is it?" Her eyebrows went up in disbelief. "What else are any of us doing? Felt like we were all just marking time. Maybe the time is now."

"And you'll talk to Verónica about starting a new run of the graphic novel?" Jake asked, signing the splash page. "Further adventures? Why did I ever let you talk me into helping your friend start a comic book about us?"

"Good publicity." Rik grinned. "How else was I going to meet the President of the United States anyway? The last one, not the current punk. He was a fan. I mean, the man's a serious nerd."

"More Pacific Force memorabilia?" Jake pressed, finishing and handing her back the stack.

He assumed that she'd get everyone's signature on this batch and make them true collectors' items.

"The same IP contracts are in place," Rik shrugged. "None of it makes us much money personally, but again, it makes others like Verónica a nice living. Plus, T-shirt makers. Lunch boxes. Action figures. Might have to commission a new set of challenge coins for this. We'll call it 'The Return.'"

"I'm glad you handle all that stuff," Jake said. "You can deal with Verónica yourself."

"She's still single, Jake," Rik leered.

"I'm sorry, but too many of them come across as needy groupies," Jake replied. "I know they aren't, but I'm looking for something else."

"What?"

"I'll know when she walks in the door."

Rather than speak, Rik nodded towards Hollyanne, snoring quietly in the corner.

Jake shrugged. They had, then they hadn't. At the time, it wasn't right for either of them. He had no idea if it might be now.

"Maybe you're right," he finally said. "This makes me feel more alive than anything I've done in the last two years. More right."

"Take him down and start hunting bad guys again?" she smiled.

"We've got to find him first," Jake reminded her. "Then stop whatever crap he's up to this time."

NATHANIEL PREFERRED DRESSING NICELY, but today they were wearing shooting clothes. Not that he was a slob, but plus four pants and argyle socks always felt weird, as did the strange shooting jacket with the patch pockets on the hips, where an American suit would have welted pockets.

They were up-country in Warwickshire, deep in some of the wilder parts of the West Midlands, although they were staying well away from Stratford-upon-Avon and Rugby.

At least he could wear a tie, even if he'd kept the nice ones back home. This was a rugged cotton one made to look like silk but sturdy enough to go through the wash. Made for hooligans wanting to look good, rather than folks that spent good money on silk ties. Blue, as always, with thin white stripes and a Brighton Seagull at the tip.

He and Tommy had over-under shotguns and ammunition to complete the look, but right now he was studying a distant spot with a pair of binoculars. He handed them to Tommy and checked the area around them.

"Not much to look at, is it?" Tommy grumbled after a second.

"That's the point," Nathaniel replied. "You don't build a secret data center and then tell everyone about it by putting up a sign and such. A simple fence with wire around it, some lights. The security will be inside."

"Can we take it?" Tommy asked, still a little askance.

"We can." Nathaniel nodded. "I just wanted one last look at the place before tomorrow. We won't be able to hide what we've done, or I'd take a slower approach and seduce our way in. As is, we'll hit it, steal backup tapes that we can decipher elsewhere, and have a whole raft of new blackmail available."

"Are there any honest politicians in Parliament?" Tommy asked with a tone midway between a sneer and a faux tear.

"A handful," Nathaniel smiled. "Mostly the young ones who are still bright-eyed innocents in the way of things. They all start cutting corners soon enough. If you own the news media, or do favors for the folks who do, there's not a lot of reason to stay clean. Plus, a lot of Russian money has come through London over the last thirty years and some of it stuck. You'd be amazed at what files the various agencies keep as insurance."

"What about Pacific Force?" Tommy asked in a harder voice. "They gonna interrupt us?"

"Jake moves too slowly, if he even comes." Nathaniel sneered now. "In the old days, he would send Grant in ahead of time to scout things out, and then slip in a week later in what is supposed to be a quiet thing, with only a few dozen groupies and news reporters at the airport. I know he's still in the game. Just a few days ago he helped the Americans with a Sino-Canadian smuggling ring, but he did so all by himself. If he tries this, we'll be ready for him."

"What about the others?"

"Still mad at Hollyanne?" Nathaniel smiled at the man.

"Caught me off guard, she did," Tommy said defensively.

"She does that," Nathaniel agreed.

He didn't need to tell the pug that she'd probably had his number for years and just never gotten a chance to prove it. Mikhail had thought that his Russian Army training made him tough. But that was only useful against drunks in bars.

Still, come to think of it, that described most of his old gang. Thugs and bullies, in spite of being well-trained killers.

But if he had to be looking over his shoulder for Jake McNeil right now, he'd feed the man to Tommy and Lucky and let them take their chances. He could always quietly slip aboard a fishing boat and pop up in Ireland, or maybe Brittany.

And maybe, just maybe it was time to upgrade his gang. Bring in some better talent at the top end. Mikhail's unfortunate departure had opened at least one slot. What other needs might he express?

"What do I tell the boys, boss?" Tommy asked, handing him back the optics.

Nathaniel slipped them into a pocket, shouldered the shotgun, and turned to take the long hike back to their car. Tommy hopped to, sliding alongside.

"It's Saturday now, and I'm sure that security around the place is probably supposed to look lax, weekend and all that," Nathaniel mused as he trudged back down the hill to the stream flowing below. "I'm not fooled. Monday morning, everyone will be settling in and on the ball, regardless of hangovers, so we'll hit them Sunday night around midnight. The backups from London and elsewhere should be done by then, so we'll have all of last week rolled up for us."

"Gonna blow up Birmingham's Council House?" Tommy asked with what Nathaniel could only classify as unholy glee.

But then, the man had done any number of unruly things both before coming into Nathaniel's employ, as well as since.

"The plan calls for a small bomb nearby to buy us time and deflect all the authorities," Nathaniel agreed. "Not the Council House, but One Chamberlain Square was only topped out last December. That means lots of construction vehicles will be moving around to confuse things. And a small bomb, Tommy. Just enough to get everyone looking that way. Understood?"

"I'll talk to me bomb maker and make sure she tones it down a bit," Tommy said. "Maybe just a suitcase in a boot or something."

"Excellent," Nathaniel agreed. "We're moving quicker than I originally wanted, but there's no reason not to do this professionally."

Tommy grunted rather than reply, which just told Nathaniel that the man had probably already lined up a couple of tons of ammonium nitrate or something equally crude and outrageous.

Nathaniel had never made it to the top of anyone's lists to have assassins come after him because he'd rarely killed innocents. The people he'd had killed always had it coming, and he'd never actually pulled the trigger himself.

A small bombing in a sensitive downtown. Noisy but generally harmless. Nothing larger than the old Quebecois blowing up mailboxes in their day, but it would get all the authorities trapped in downtown Birmingham in a sea of confusion and bad traffic while he was just over this hill metaphorically, stealing the heart and soul of British Intelligence and using it to refresh all his old blackmail files.

Nathaniel was so happy to be back in business.

CHAPTER
NINE

GRANT LOOKED around the restaurant as he walked in. It was a tourist kind of joint, specializing in fish and chips for those folks wanting an *Authentic Experience* to take home with them.

Well, close enough to authentic. Not many locals ate here, but that might just be because of all the foreigners with bad manners. The man in the corner behind the counter was Pakistani originally, although he'd been here nearly forever at this point. Enough to be a fixture even the most ardently racist EDL punks generally ignored. And the English Defense League hated everybody.

Murad didn't give two shits about the EDL. Or anyone else.

The man looked up at Grant now, caught his gaze, and jerked his head around back with the faintest motion. Grant slid to the far end of the counter and around, heading into a hallway where restrooms were located. Murad was a step ahead of him and paused to size Grant up.

"Hungry?" the man asked.

"Famished," Grant nodded.

Murad leaned out to speak to a young woman walking

close by. Possibly a great niece, but Grant wasn't sure beyond a vague family resemblance.

"Bring a plate down," he ordered the young woman and then unlocked a door into the cellar, leading the way.

Tap room, or something like that. Lots of kegs down here along two walls, along with a space in the corner that had been set up as an office. Murad sat behind the desk and gestured to a chair.

As Grant sat, Murad pulled two glasses from a shelf and uncovered a small tap in the wall behind him. He filled both with that nut brown ale that Murad liked and handed one to Grant.

"You didn't call first," Murad began with a smile and an accent so East London that you could almost etch glass with it. "What brings you to London?"

"I only got my own call a little over twenty-four hours ago," Grant smiled. "Was in Toronto. Apparently, things are happening in London."

"Ivanov," Murad nodded.

He stopped speaking as the door to the cellar opened. Grant saw a hand disappear out of sight behind the desk and assumed that the man was holding a pistol, just in case.

Murad had a lot of friends. Most of his enemies were dead.

The young woman from before appeared with a plate in one hand, several pieces of breaded fish and a stack of chips. She put it down in front of Grant silently, along with napkins and a bottle of malt vinegar, nodded to both of them, and departed back up the stairs.

At no point had she smiled.

Still, the fish was fresh out of the oil. Grant grabbed a piece, thought better of it, and dropped it to cool before he blistered his fingers.

"Ivanov?" Grant prompted once he heard the door upstairs close again.

"Dead Russian mercenary, not that far from here," Murad said. "Just across the river. A couple of vague inquiries from toffs asking if I'd done it, but nothing serious. No clue who dropped him."

"Jake thinks that Nathaniel Hoestler never left England," Grant replied. "Everyone else does, but Ivanov here suggests that maybe Jake's right."

"Pacific Force back in business?" Murad perked up.

That would be a useful tidbit of information to sell on, at least until it became general knowledge. And it would stir up a few hornet nests when it got out.

Not an accident that Grant had started here, though.

"Quietly," Grant agreed. "Hunting right now, because the information is several days old at this point, and the man could have gone anywhere."

"Am I your goat?" Murad smiled.

Grant figured his fish had cooled enough. He blew on it and took a bite, thankful for the ale to cool it some more.

"Somebody might as well get a few favors out of the information," Grant offered. "If Hoestler is still around, the underground will twitch pretty hard, knowing Jake and the team are coming."

The man laughed now.

"What information are you looking for?" Murad asked.

"Who might be a target big enough to keep Hoestler in-country?" Grant said. "Or what?"

"London's locked down pretty hard right now," Murad mused. "Couple of rumors of Provisional IRA rogues running around, looking for mischief. That sort of thing."

"Rogues?" Grant asked.

"I think one of them is a bombmaker, but I don't know too much," Murad said, then corrected himself. "Not yet, anyway. Would be useful to know if we're about to have another round of craziness hit."

"Jake wants to keep things quiet," Grant offered.

"Might not be Jake's decision," Murad said with a sad smile. "Thought things had gotten quiet finally when Jake put him in prison. Shame they couldn't keep him."

"We're going to put him back," Grant said, his voice dropping to a tone to convey seriousness, even as he munched on his fish.

"The young woman you saw was Senzala," Murad said. "My grandniece. When you call, if I am not available, ask for her by name and identify yourself as the man in the cellar. She'll be able to tell you if we know anything."

"That smart?" Grant asked, a bit taken back.

"She'll end up owning the place when I die," Murad said. "Her mother and siblings are hard workers, but none of them are smart enough to be successful in this business. Either of them."

"I see," Grant nodded.

Murad dabbled in things on both sides of the law. The restaurant would be easy enough to run. But the other things would take a special touch. And brains.

"You sit here and eat," Murad said, rising with his glass in hand. "I'll make a few calls and will maybe know something before you leave."

He went up the stairs and closed the door behind him, leaving Grant alone.

Grant ate the lovely meal, tracking a variety of topics in his head to see where he should go next. Murad was the best contact for what Grant was looking for, but not the only one.

But something was definitely going on around here. It stank bad enough that Grant could smell it over the oil and fish he was devouring.

CHAPTER
TEN

ENGLAND. Nice morning though a bit blustery. Green fields they'd flown over as the sun came up. There were even sheep visible in the distance, placidly munching the grass.

Jake nodded to the sheep then looked around the parking lot, standing out front of the hangar where the jet had parked. They had the space largely to themselves, Hollyanne watching every direction and Spencer typing something on his phone. Rik was approaching now, driving an old Rover they were borrowing from another friend, just pulling up to the curb in front of him.

He popped around the back and opened the rear door.

"You brought the guitar case?" Jake called to the front of the idling vehicle.

Rik smiled at him in the rear-view mirror as Jake and Spencer started loading suitcases and bags.

"We're supposed to declare it with customs," Jake said. "You know that."

"It is *not* a firearm," Rik replied tartly. "The law is exceptionally specific on firearms and rather vague everywhere else."

He supposed she was right. Anyone smuggling a take-down recurve bow in a guitar case had probably read those statutes closely. He grunted and slipped into the front seat, unconsciously expecting a steering wheel since he was on the left side.

But this was England. And Rik was driving.

"Rik, you've got directions to the place we're renting?" Spencer asked from the back as they pulled away.

Customs had been a great deal less rigorous than it might have been coming through a commercial airport. Jake tried not to take advantage of that too often, but Pacific Force, arriving in a private jet, let him slip around certain things.

Like slipping the agent a hundred pounds and asking her not to type her paperwork into the national system until Monday. Two days' head start on Nathaniel and whoever else might make all the difference.

"So why are we staying in Birmingham?" Rik asked as she got them onto surface streets and headed towards the M6.

"It's central," Jake replied, watching cars around him. In spite of a call from Perkins over the Atlantic, he was still a little wound up from the chase on Thursday that had ended with Perkins rounding up the last four stragglers. "We can get to London quickly, but I doubt that Nathaniel is still lurking in the City. Liverpool, Manchester, Leeds, and the North are all handy, if we need to go that way."

"Why not down to Brighton?" Hollyanne asked from the back.

"If there was a bigger trap, I'm not sure what it might be," Jake laughed. "That town's too small for us to not end up running into someone on the other side who would recognize at least one of us. Birmingham is large enough we can be anonymous if we work a little."

"But we still assume he's in England?" Rik asked, swerving around some of the weekend traffic.

"Between the message I read and someone dumping Ivanov, I think it is a safe enough bet," Spencer chimed in. "We've gone over the logic."

"Yeah, but that was yesterday," Rik laughed. "You know how things change in this business."

That got a laugh. Sometimes, plans lasted all of five minutes before you ended up blowing it all up and freelancing a solution. That was what made Pacific Force work. He could trust all of them with his life, and they him.

Someone would always come up with a solution.

***

JAKE HAD TOLD Spencer to go small. They had a large house with a two-week rental and option for at least another two weeks after that, although Jake assumed at this point that if they didn't find Nathaniel by then that he had truly gone to ground, and it would be time to return to Seattle. Then they'd have to spend time and money grinding after leads and leakers.

Everyone was settled and they had gathered in the living room. There was a pool in the backyard, almost American style, but the weather was cool verging on cold. Only Hollyanne would be crazy enough to swim. The afternoon was dragging into dinnertime.

His phone rang. Grant. He'd programmed the burner number already.

"Might have a lead," the man said as Jake answered.

"Talk to me," Jake replied, putting Grant on speaker so everyone could listen in.

Around him, everyone perked up, Rik going so far as

to empty her bottle of Starbucks mocha in one breath, just in case.

"According to whispers, London has been quiet for a while," Grant continued. "But something or somebody has been stirring the pot lately. Outsiders, at least according to my regular contacts."

"Nathaniel?" Jake asked.

"As likely as anybody," Grant agreed. "Locals don't like the whispers going around. Suggestions and hints of pending violence, which always brings the authorities down hard on everyone else."

"What do you need from us?" Jake pressed.

"I think, and this is just a gut reaction, but I think maybe we need a strong-arm job tonight," Grant said.

"Where?"

"Here in London," Grant said. "Got a lead out by Camden Town on the way to Kentish. Freelance bomb maker who's been working lately. Ordering supplies and things like that."

"Big?" Rik spoke up.

"Got supplied more than she needed for simple party favors, according to one contact who wished to remain blameless when it all went down."

"Do we alert the authorities?" Hollyanne asked now.

"She's got former IRA connections, so that would turn into an evening news shit show," Grant replied. "Too much smoke and I think we'd lose the flame in the confusion."

"Is she in motion?" Jake asked.

"Hard to tell," Grant said. "Orders for supplies that got delivered earlier this week, but I got the impression she worked fast, so maybe? That's why we might take her out now. Maybe we catch her making the bomb. If not, maybe we get a lead on who did it."

"We're in Birmingham now, close to Solihull," Jake said. "We can be there in two to three hours."

"Capital," Grant replied, giving them an address in the northern part of London. "We'll meet there and then have a quick reconnoiter of the target's flat."

"Should I bring my guitar, Grant?" Rik asked.

There was a long pause. Grant would not be surprised that the woman was armed. That was one of her normal jobs, with Spencer as her spotter when Jake needed ranged firepower brought to bear. Normally a high-powered hunting rifle or maybe something heavier. Grant was usually either well away, or perhaps right up front, fast-talking his way in a door while trusting that Rik and the others had his back.

"Probably not the worst idea," Grant finally said. "They'd appreciate a little Robin Hood mixed with Lady Godiva around here."

"I'll be dressed, you goof." Rik laughed with the rest of them.

"A man can dream, can't he?" Grant said.

They got off the phone quickly, and Jake looked around the room.

"Strongarm?" Hollyanne asked.

"You're on point," Jake nodded. "I'll trail and cover your wing. Rik and Spencer will watch. Grant will either need to knock, or he can sit back with the others and keep watch."

"Do we tell anyone we're going in?" Spencer asked now.

Jake considered it. They weren't supposed to go around the authorities, but usually did. Jake didn't need warrants or approvals from Home Secretaries to act. That was part of Pacific Force's edge.

Plus, the current Government had proven itself more

than a little inimical to private vigilante groups. And they leaked like a rusty pipe. Jake wondered how much Russian money had been propping up the Tories lately now that they were in the process of destroying the last vestiges of the Once-Mighty British Empire.

"No," he decided after a moment. "Spencer, you make sure you're monitoring police frequencies. Maybe hack into the CCTV system so we have cameras on our target. But be prepared to shut down their whole system if you have to."

"Brought my little black bag for just such an occasion," Spencer said with an evil smile. "Need to swing by a spot and chat with a friend on our way in. Owe him a favor and it's on our way."

"As long as he doesn't know what we're about," Jake warned. "It's just us going in."

"Oh, he's one of us," Spencer assured him.

Jake was mostly mollified by that. They all had friends with questionable backgrounds, but everyone Pacific Force worked with had been vetted.

They were already walking on a narrow ledge.

CHAPTER
ELEVEN

RIK GAVE off watching the flat across the way and ducked back down behind the low wall to look over at Spencer. It was night, so odds were low that anyone would see them, but that was no reason to take chances.

"Two questions," she said. "First, how did you talk that guy into letting you borrow his entire camera rig for the night? And second, can that thing really see in the dark, or were you planning to beat someone to death with it?"

Spencer looked up from the bag he'd been rifling through and placed a possessive hand on the camera with the long lens on the front.

"You know anything about cameras?" he asked.

"No." She snorted. "You know that. I can maybe get my phone to take some reasonable pictures, but that's it."

"Sure," Spencer nodded back. "D-SLR means digital, single lens reflex. Highest end stuff you can buy. I have this one set up for surveillance, so the biggest telephoto lens, and the light-gathering is good enough that I can take pictures in her window from here or shift and catch someone moving outside. The other one in the bag is more for portrait work. You know: up close, well lit, nobody moving. Evidence sorts of things, although we don't usually need that."

"And he's letting you play with all his expensive hardware without him standing right there?" Rik teased. "I know how you people are with your toys."

"Any pictures I take, Josh and I are sharing ownership later," Spencer grinned. "Jake will need some of them for evidence, but not all. The rest Josh can sell to newspapers once we're done. Being that it *is* Pacific Force, those will sell and make him money while I get credit. It works out, like you and the comic books with Verónica."

"Huh," Rik decided. "All right, what can you see from here?"

"I was just about to find out," he said, coming upright from where he was kneeling. "Usually, you need a tripod or something when shooting at night, but I won't be using a flash, so it shouldn't get jittery. Got your headset on?"

Rik checked the earpiece and adjusted the mic a little.

"Testing one two," she said.

"Clear here," Spencer replied.

"Same here," Jake also said.

"I hear you," Hollyanne piped up.

Rik popped up like a meercat now but stayed low. She had her blond locks tied back loosely and had a light-colored knit cap on to break up her silhouette against the stone coaming.

The target flat was across a wide street and down a little. They were on a roof one floor higher with a reasonable view into a living room. Rik assumed that the bedroom with the curtains drawn contained a small workshop, since someone was watching TV in the living room. She could see legs, but not anything more from her vantage.

But her job wasn't watching. Or rather, not just watching. She had assembled her bow from the guitar case and strung it. For travel, it broke down into three pieces: a center and two arms that got bolted down with a big Allen wrench. She had a nifty toy to string it, hooking it and the string over one end, and then pulling a loop over the far end to rest on the stave itself. You stood up and it bowed everything to the point you could attach the string and be done.

Not her highest tech bow, as it only had a whisker biscuit on the side for holding the shaft of an arrow. Back home, she had a much heavier compound bow with illuminated pin sights, a peep sight, and various attachments and modifications to silence the string and the wheels.

London made far more noise than the Cascade Mountains, even at night. And her target wasn't a nervous deer or elk. Hell, the elevation might remind people of a tree stand, but if she had to shoot through that window over there, that was barely a six-foot drop.

More interesting would be going after a target on the ground, with a four-story drop and a long, slanting angle, depending on which way the rabbit turned when she hit the bottom of the stairwell. No wind tonight, which helped.

"One female, in the living room, seated," Spencer said quietly over the channel he had secured. "No one else visible, but the lights are on in the bedroom at present. What's the perimeter look like?"

"A couple of folks either coming from a pub or headed to one," Rik said, turning right and left. "Parked cars everywhere. Adequate lighting. No other watchers I've been able to see."

"Good," Spencer said. "Interior team?"

"We're just outside the back in an alley, waiting for you," Jake said. "Grant nods that he is ready to make his approach, but doesn't have comm."

Which made sense. If he was supposed to walk up to someone's door and knock, he needed to look like a guy with a bag of takeout food that had written down the wrong address. Jake and Hollyanne would be covering him.

"Standby, I have movement in the apartment," Spencer suddenly said louder as the camera began to click. "Female subject has risen and moved to the hallway. Stopped. Talking to someone in back."

"Conversation or yelling at a dog?" Hollyanne asked.

"Uhm, conversational interludes, I think," Spencer said.

Rik shifted around her arrow a bit. She had four with lead tips that were blunt on the end and about the size of a quarter. Awkward and short ranged, even shooting from a roof, but they hit like a baseball when you did it right.

Next to that, she had one with a hollow tip and paint. That stuff was lime green and also fluoresced hard under black light in case someone started to run, and you needed to track them.

Rik picked up the one that was one of her favorite inventions. Steel tip, hardened and ground down to a sharp point. Behind that was a small chemical igniter and a tube of modified gunpowder. Shot it through a window or something hard enough to set it off, wait one second, and you had a pocket flash-bang good enough to blind anyone in a room and usually stun them. Blew the arrow apart, but they were cheap shafts she picked up by the dozen online anyway.

Two people or more suggested the need for a hard distraction when the team at the door got aggressive. Up until now, Rik had been expecting maybe a runner she needed to trip with a corner shot, like banking the eight ball.

"Sniper, ready to flash-bang the room," she announced quietly as she nocked that arrow and rose from her crouch to a slumped standing position, staves horizontal now but fast enough to get vertical if she stood to shoot.

This was not her first rodeo.

"Female target is moving to the front door now," Spencer said, clicking more photos. "Do we approach and intercept or let her escape containment and engage separately?"

"Is the other person visible?" Hollyanne asked.

"Negative," Spencer replied. "Feels like someone just got sent to the corner market for something. She's putting on a jacket now."

"Shit," Hollyanne muttered. "Okay, Team One will engage her outside the apartment. Team Two and Sniper be prepared to penetrate the space."

Rik nodded to herself. Hollyanne and Grant would accost the woman. Jake would either knock on the door or kick it in. Either way, Rik needed to be ready to switch targets quickly. She glanced down and placed the stun-tip arrows in her mind.

Spencer kept up a running commentary, but Rik tuned him out. He was just doing play-by-play at this point. She remained focused on the sliding glass door in front of her. And the need to shoot.

"Female is out of my sight," Spencer announced. "Will maintain observation on second target."

Rik smiled.

Somebody was in for a rude surprise shortly.

HOLLYANNE HAD HOPED that they could walk right up on the target and trap her in her flat. Easier to control someone that way. Here, she and Grant were outside the front door of the building, out of position to catch her even in the stairwell, assuming she went this way. Jake had the back stairs, and it was a crapshoot.

"Drop the bags and pretend we're on a date," Hollyanne muttered to Grant.

She took his hand in hers, and they emerged from the alley onto the sidewalk and started towards the front door, not quite jogging but moving quickly.

In her head, a clock was ticking, but then, it almost always was when violence was on the menu.

They got to the front of the building and opened the door. Foyer with black and white tile floors that needed to be updated. Old wood walls stained nearly black with age and shoulders brushing against them.

Wood steps up on her right, but she didn't hear anyone coming down. Maybe the female was silent. Maybe she had gone down the back.

Hollyanne wanted to take the steps two at a time like a

military operation, but she kept herself tightly controlled, holding Grant's hand like two lovers coming home from a few pints and about to screw each other's brains out as loudly as possible. At least that was the look she hoped she had on her face.

Grant's plastic face was innocence itself, but he did that. She smiled and he turned into a Lothario before her eyes with a grin.

Second floor. Nothing, so they kept going. Maybe she was moving slow?

No. Hollyanne heard a tussle over the headset.

Damn it, the woman had gone down the back stairs and run into Jake.

Hopefully, he could control the situation.

Hollyanne needed to kick a door in.

JAKE ENTERED the rear of the building, off a small yard that connected the backs of several buildings and had probably been something of a park before it got cobbled over into an ugly parking lot.

This door had the look of more of a servant's entrance, small and dingy. The sort of place you might slink in quietly in the morning with an embarrassed slut walk, regardless of gender. These stairs were narrower than the ones up front. Maybe six feet wide instead of ten. Old wood, bowed a little in the middle. Walls instead of being open to the air like the front.

The air stank of curry and kimchi that had been too many dinners around here.

Jake got to the second floor quickly and had just turned to head up the next flight when he caught the sound of someone coming down. One person. Alone. Moving quickly but not trying to be silent. Not running, either, so much as bopping down the stairs on their way somewhere.

This was where Jake was at a disadvantage. Nobody knew what the woman looked like except Spencer. He'd seen her through the window. Maybe Rik as well.

All Jake knew was that his target was a female. And no longer contained in her flat.

He took a deep breath and let himself flow into preparation for a combat state, just in case. He'd hoped that the woman would go down the front, where Hollyanne had help to take her down.

Jake started up the steps like he had just finished a long day on the docks and needed to change before a hard night of drinking. Kind of slumped and hunched. Growly.

A woman was coming down the stairs as he looked up. Hard thirty or a reasonable fifty, it was hard to tell. A little pudgy around the middle, with extra hips and thighs. She wore jeans and a black cotton jacket zipped up against the wind and chill outside.

Brown hair once, but mostly stringy gray now, shoulder length where it had escaped the hair band holding most of it back. Her face was just irregular enough to be homely without being ugly.

Hazel eyes locked on him as they were about fifteen feet apart but closing rapidly. She blinked and her step faltered.

"You," she gasped.

There were downsides to being famous as a crime fighter. Sometimes the bad guys know who you are before you know them.

The woman reached for a back pocket. Jake guessed she was going for a gun.

He moved, charging up the steps at her. There wasn't any space to maneuver in here, and he had specifically not brought a gun with him tonight. Or even to England. There were ways and people if he needed one, but this was just a contract connection.

She had a gun, though. Her motion was obvious as her right hand went back. The jacket probably saved his life, as she couldn't get it up and over the gun fast enough to draw it.

Fighting on stairsteps was another interesting way to dance. Her weight was back. where her right leg was still up a step, and her shoulders were turned almost sideways now.

He needed to make sure he didn't end up throwing her down a staircase and breaking her neck.

Jake snapped out his right hand to knock her left hand up and away, punching up into her stomach with his left.

The woman fell onto her bottom and that jarred the gun loose. Thankfully, it didn't fire when it dropped out of her hand. You never knew with cheap guns.

Apparently, she had studied close combat somewhere, because the woman kicked out from where she sat on the step, and Jake took it on his hip and thigh, staggering him to his right.

If he gave her any opening, she'd have that gun, so he lunged at the woman, striking with a fist and elbow, but she got both her hands and a knee up to block, almost curling into a ball like an armadillo to keep him at bay.

Jake shifted as she blocked, trying to shove her now, letting the ball shape work in his favor long enough that he could get to the gun and disable it. Or just disable her.

She wasn't going to fall for it, though, springing out to put both feet flat on a step and grabbing at him. This woman had no reason to keep him alive, so Jake had to protect himself.

They ended up tangled like dancers or lovers, almost nose to nose for a moment as hands shifted. She'd studied martial arts as well as he had, and similar ones. Each grip was immediately blocked. Every elbow met a shoulder or a forearm. Knees blocked.

She went to head butt him, but Jake saw it coming as

she reared back, so he leaned his weight back sideways on the step and pulled instead.

He collapsed his knees just enough that when he leaned back, he was able to bounce the woman's face off the sheetrock instead of his nose. Hers might have broken. There was blood, at least, flowing freely.

Jake let go long enough to rabbit punch her from his lower position, shifting to put his own butt on a step and getting leverage. She grunted and lashed out with a fist that connected enough with his ear to sting. Fortunately, she was on the wrong side to break his headset or drive it into his ear, but he needed to pay attention to keep that out of her reach.

He had a hand on her side, just behind and below her left breast. Jake put his other hand on her bottom and shoved her flat into the wall and down another step.

She needed to be kept away from the gun. If nothing else, Hollyanne could get here at some point, so the woman needed to be disarmed.

He grabbed for the gun, and the woman jumped on his back, pummeling his ribs with punches.

Jake snapped an elbow back, but she blocked it. It did overbalance her, though, and she fell onto her side.

The gun was out of reach unless he wanted to get hit some more, so Jake rolled with her like a gator, coming up and over and ending up between her legs, as if they had stopped to shag right in the stairwell like a couple of drunks.

The woman wrapped her legs tight around his hips now to hold him in range, while she started punching and striking again. She had an advantage for leverage, but he had her pinned in place and didn't try to do anything but tire her out.

Instead, he planted his toes on a step and thrust

forward, driving his hips into hers. She bounced off the wood with a curse that should have moved them down the steps some, but Jake wasn't feeling like a caring lover. He humped her harder, squishing the woman's head and shoulders into a step and hunching her over.

Ought to be getting hard to breathe, as many punches as she had been throwing. Jake was gasping like a bellows from the effort.

She finally made a mistake. Small one, but one nonetheless. Two expert fighters, well matched.

The woman turned and reached for the gun, resting tantalizingly close on the step next to them as they fought.

Her right hand. Jake's left side. She turned her chest that way to bring her left hand and arm in to protect, so he reared back a little and let her, just enough to throw a hard right cross into her ear.

In boxing, that's a good stinger, because of all the nerves right there. Her head had nowhere to rebound to, so he drove her skull into the step instead.

Sounded painful from the dull, echoing thud. Her movements staggered, so he shifted down and began punishing her ribs again. They needed this woman alive, not curb-stomped.

But she was woozy, even as her hand closed on the weapon.

Jake reached over and wrapped his larger hand over hers and picked both up just enough to slam her hand and the gun into the step. A second time. A third, and she dropped it.

He was already leaned over that way with her, so Jake reared back again as her legs loosened, but only to back-hand her across the center of her jaw with the back of his fist, knuckles first.

She went out like a light.

Jake finally grabbed the gun and heaved himself upright to study the woman.

Damn, she was tough.

"Maybe you two should get a room?" a voice asked.

Jake spun with the pistol ready to fire, but it was only Hollyanne, grinning as she crossed to him.

"Where's Grant?" he gasped, finally able to draw a good breath in.

"Watching the apartment with Rik," she said.

Jake moved to one side and collapsed his hurt ass onto the step. Hollyanne pulled out a pocketful of zip ties and proceeded to truss the woman up like a turkey.

"Now what?" he asked.

This was still her op. He'd put her in charge, so he'd listen.

"Now, you and Grant get her to the Rover and put her under that blanket in back after I frisk her for everything," Hollyanne replied, pulling out a key ring with a wicked smile. "Then Grant watches her while you and I commit felony breaking and entering. Works?"

"Works," Jake said.

He staggered upright, glad that he'd had the weight to hold the woman down. Mean and tough.

Almost too much to handle.

But only almost.

HOLLYANNE HAD RELIEVED Grant and sent him down to help Jake get their supposed bombmaker out to the truck. Whoever she was, armed with a firearm and attacking on sight was a dead giveaway in this business. Now, Jake was back with her, and they were on either side of the target door, flat against the wall out of sight of the peephole.

No sounds around them, but it was late on a Saturday night. Not so late that people would be staggering home soon, but everyone going out had already left.

She nodded to Jake and moved quickly to the door, slipping the key in the lock. He still had the woman's gun, but that was mostly a prop at this point. The last thing she wanted was gunfire around bombs or making materials.

"Making entry now," she announced to the team over the tac comm.

Hollyanne opened the door in a smooth movement and went right through. Rik hadn't seen the other target emerge from the back, so they'd need to get to whoever it was fast. Spencer had described the interior, so Hollyanne moved quickly.

Past the entry hallway and living space. By the kitchen and tiny dining nook that smelled of fried pork and rancid bacon grease. There was a hallway ahead that led to two bedrooms and a bath, if she had to guess.

"You back early?" a male voice called querulously from the last door on the left.

Hollyanne grunted something non-committal and moved faster. Almost running, but still quiet.

A hand closed on the handle from inside as she approached. Hollyanne watched it turn and start to open. Rather than ask, she just exploded into the door itself, knocking whoever it was on his ass and surging into the bedroom.

Not a bedroom. Shit. Full bomb laboratory. Man on his ass, stunned. Couple of what might be pipe bombs on the shelf nearby.

Hollyanne dropped her whole weight, what little of it there was, down onto the man, cracking him with a tight cross falling. Just to be sure, she punched him in the balls as hard as she could as well once she was on top of him.

Sounded almost like a rabbit she had heard once after it had been mauled by a coyote she had accidentally chased off, that high squeal that cut through everything.

"Other doors," Hollyanne snapped back over her shoulder at Jake as she hit her target a third time.

He'd curled into a ball, so she went after his left mastoid process, all those nerves clustered behind his ear. He was out cold after that.

Hollyanne rolled the man over and zip tied his hands behind him and then his feet. A frisk revealed a folding knife she took and another pistol like the one Jake was holding.

"Clear," Jake called a moment later.

Good. The one thing she'd feared was three people

here instead of two, and Jake having to shoot someone. No way to keep this raid quiet at that point, even if the locals wouldn't complain too loudly once they took a look in here.

Hollyanne grabbed the mutt by his feet and started dragging him into the front room, just to get him away from all these toys. Wasn't that hard. The girl was built solid, but this guy was lanky and short. Younger, but just as rough, and you didn't get tattoos like the one on his neck anywhere but a Russian prison.

In the living room, she spun him around so that Spencer could get a good picture and then added some ties to hook him to the coffee table. The man could still break it to get loose, but he wasn't going to threaten Jake with a gun on him.

"He's yours," she told Jake.

Hollyanne returned to the bedroom studio and studied it.

"Spencer, I'm going to open some curtains so you can get pictures," she announced. "Then I'm going to shoot some with my phone. How soon do we call someone about a place like this and blow it all over the news?"

"How bad is it?" Jake asked from the front room.

"Small," she replied. "Pipe bombs. Briefcase-scale, maybe. Nothing truck-scale."

"I probably need to look," Spencer chimed in. "Gimme five minutes and I'll knock three times."

"See you shortly," Hollyanne replied.

She didn't want to touch anything in here. Spencer was the most versed on Explosives Ordinance, but none of them really dealt with bombs that much. Even Nathaniel had only used simple stuff and then mostly to threaten hostages.

Blowing up a building would have gotten all the intelligence agencies in the world coming after him. Nathaniel Hoestler was really an electronic con artist in the grand scheme of things. He didn't want to make anyone's *Top 1000 Enemies of the State* list.

That was a recipe for a sniper shooting him through a window someday.

However, chances were, he'd hired these two for something.

What was that man wanting to blow up?

CHAPTER
FIFTEEN

SPENCER JOGGED across the dark street and into the front door of the apartment building. He'd left the monster camera with Rik and grabbed the one better suited for portraiture work, as he'd be in the well-lit indoors taking stills. Sounded like time to gather evidence and intelligence against the next part of the mission.

"Grant, how's the girl?" he asked as he entered the foyer and started up the stairs.

"A little grumpy, but the BDSM scene seems to suit her," Grant replied.

Good. Bound. Gagged. Blindfolded. She'd seen Jake, but Spencer doubted that the man Hollyanne had taken down could recognize her, from the sounds of things. They would just need to find out what she knew and then hand her off to one of Grant's friends.

Up the stairs, Spencer was struck by both how empty it was, and how it managed to convey squalor without ever quite embracing it. If they would repaint the walls and scrub the floors really hard even once, the landlord could probably significantly raise the rents. Maybe attract a higher class of losers to live here, rather than folks building bombs and whatever else the locals might discover if they chose to just swarm the place one morning and inspect every flat simultaneously.

He got to the fourth floor and looked both ways, but the hallway was empty, so he emerged, took a quick photo just to anchor every shot after this, and approached the door. He knocked three times quietly and waited.

No steps approached, but Jake and Hollyanne moved like ghosts when they were on a mission. That was part of the reason Spencer was usually with Rik. In addition to being her spotter, he wasn't that quiet. Only sort of clumsy.

The door opened and Jake stopped pointing a gun at him, which was a relief.

"Hey, who are you?" a voice on his right suddenly called out.

Spencer turned and made eye contact with a man who must have come up the back stairs. He gave the impression of tall and kind of beefy. Dark in a Slavic sort of way. Dressed like a bouncer maybe, in heavy pants and a baggy jacket.

"Shit," the man grunted.

He turned and bolted back into the stairwell.

"We've got a runner," Spencer announced.

"Move," Jake ordered, blasting by him already at a dead run. "Keep up."

That made sense. Jake hadn't seen him, so he couldn't identify the man.

Spencer started after Jake, trailing by a few steps already and falling farther behind.

"Eastern European male," Spencer said calmly as he tried to keep up. "Dark clothes. Big boy but not fat. Going down the back stairs. Jake and I are in pursuit."

Jake was a whole floor ahead when Spencer got to the stairwell and started down. He could hear the other man approaching the ground floor already, so that man must have leapt off every landing or something.

Spencer put his head down and ran.

CHAPTER
SIXTEEN

JAKE COULD HEAR THE TARGET. The man was obviously running for his life.

Jake considered the words of one of Nathaniel's thugs, early in the life of Pacific Force.

"I only have to run scared faster than you can run angry, mate," the man had said.

Fool had tried. Failed, but tried. Jake would give him that.

Jake started running scared. If this one got away, their cover would be blown, and Nathaniel would know he was in town with the whole team. Felt like they were already at a dangerous junction of the game right now, so he flew down the stairs, leaving Spencer way behind.

"Target running for the front door," Jake called, hoping that maybe Grant could intercept him or at least slow the man down a little.

Jake got to the ground floor and gave chase. He was slowly gaining, as the runner was only now getting to the front door. Unless something happened, he ought to catch the man in two or three blocks.

But something always happened in a chase like this. A

car turning. A dog lunging. Maybe even a couple staggering out of a bar.

"Turned right," Jake said as he watched the man descend the outside step and run.

Jake exploded out of the front door and went down the six stairs in two steps, letting a parked car provide a parkour platform for him to deflect off.

The runner was half a block down when the night sky lit up with a flash that blinded Jake. The snap of an angry dragon slamming his tail onto the street hit a moment later.

Jake blinked and ran, unsure of what had just happened.

At least bad luck occasionally cut both ways.

He didn't recognize the sound the first time, but that was the surprise of the small explosion.

The runner had been staggered to a ragged halt by the flash and the sound. Now, an arrow slammed into his shoulder and knocked him to one knee. A second arrow an eyeblink later knocked the man onto his face.

Jake had forgotten about Rik in his excitement. She hadn't forgotten about him, just kept quiet as she concentrated.

Jake supposed that the man wasn't any more dangerous than the deer she went and caught every fall.

"Grab my arrows," she said as Jake got to the man.

Nasty ones, with the blunt tip made of rubber and backed with lead to give it heft. The flash had been her interpretation of a flash-bang grenade, but not as big. Still just right to surprise the hell out of everyone.

"Thank you," Jake said as he grabbed the two.

The third shaft—the flash-bang—was just shards. If he needed everything to be utterly secret, he'd grab the feathers, but this had gotten too big to just sweep under the rug.

Jake grabbed the man, rolled him over, and zip tied him. Wallet and another gun got confiscated.

Why are you people armed? This isn't the US.

But he'd need to interrogate them off-site.

Spencer was just emerging as Jake got the runner in a fireman carry.

"You go help Hollyanne and get pictures," Jake said. "I'll add this one to Grant's menagerie."

"Got it," Spencer replied, turning and moving immediately.

"Grant, call your buddy," Hollyanne broke in on the line now. "Get him here now but tell him only two people total until they talk to us."

Jake wanted to say something, but he'd put her in charge, so he shut up and trudged.

At least nobody questioned a man carrying another down the street, but London had a reputation for drunks. A real buddy was the guy who could carry a bloke home when you got blackout drunk.

Jake hauled his latest catch to the Rover and put him in the back seat. The girl was probably going with them, but the two men could be handed over to the authorities for fun when this was all done.

Grant hung up his call and smiled.

"So apparently we have a rep." Grant laughed. "They were standing by closer to the City with several teams handy, but Steve and his partner will be here in twenty minutes."

Jake smiled. Pacific Force was back, in town, and hunting. Of course, the smart money would be prepared.

Jake just wondered what anthill they had kicked over.

SPENCER REALLY NEEDED A BOMB EXPERT, but he'd learned enough over the years to agree with Hollyanne's assessment. Provocations and maybe assassinations, but not wholesale terrorism events. A little meaner than the old Quebecois separatists, but not much.

Back home, it was the sort of thing you used to blow up stumps or lose hands in the wrong neighborhoods. But this was England. Even the Irish Republican Army had built bigger things, to say nothing of splinter groups like those Provisional IRA lunatics. Not counting personality squabbles, at least the war was largely over, assuming that Brexit didn't screw it all up by introducing a hard border around Northern Ireland.

That would just undo everything pretty quickly.

Spencer took pictures of things without touching. You never knew with folks like this when they might have a booby-trap that they didn't mention to outsiders. He did make a note to recruit an on-call expert. Since Pacific Force was back in business, they'd probably need one.

Best if you could actually send live video to someone who knew what they were talking about.

"Anything?" Hollyanne asked from the door.

"No, but I don't know what I'm looking for, either," he replied, clicking and zooming.

It would all go into evidence somewhere, but they would need records as well.

"Hey, what's that?" Spencer muttered to himself as he saw what looked like blueprints.

"What have you got?" Hollyanne asked.

Spencer zoomed rather than stepped in, but he couldn't make it out. Instead, he had to walk over there, careful not to touch anything. He let the camera settle on the strap and studied the paper. Bombmakers didn't usually work with plans of their bombs. If you were that good, you did all the math and wiring in your head and just assembled things.

Blueprints suggested a building they were wanting to blow up, but nothing in this room suggested that scale.

"Grant, talk to me about the woman," Spencer spoke into the mic now. "What's her rep on the streets?"

"Pro," Grant replied instantly. "Not Irish but a sympathizer who got radicalized by parents who were fans of the Baader–Meinhof Group in the old days. What are you looking for?"

"She blow up buildings?" Spencer asked. "Like Oklahoma or the World Trade Center the first time?"

"Not that I heard," Grant replied. "Someone would have mentioned. She did small things. Why?"

"I've got blueprints to a place that looks like Birmingham," Spencer said.

"Where?" Jake asked

"One Chamberlain Square," Spencer replied.

"Still under construction, but they are getting close to done," Jake said. "Maybe a distraction?"

"For what?" Hollyanne chimed in now.

"You set off a small bomb in Birmingham, you'll have everyone looking that way," Jake said. "This is Nathaniel we're talking about. He never does anything by direct action. Always gets you looking at the wrong hand. What are we missing?"

"Guys, car pulling up," Grant called. "Looks like Steve. I assume several more back a few blocks, ready to swoop. What's the play?"

"Jake?" Hollyanne asked.

Like her, Spencer understood that this had just passed out of tactical control, so Jake should be the one making decisions now. Spencer snapped another fast round of pictures from close up.

"I'm going to bring Steve up," Jake announced. "The other one can stay down here with Grant and guard things. See you in a few."

"Got it," Spencer agreed.

It was Nathaniel. What were they missing?

CHAPTER
EIGHTEEN

JAKE RECOGNIZED the man who introduced himself as Steve today. He'd been a Charles and a Johnathon other times. The other man, the driver, was sitting in the Rover with Grant, babysitting those two. Now, he and Steve were ascending the stairs again.

Jake just hoped that he was done with close combat for tonight.

"Is there a reason you wouldn't allow us to come in heavy?" Steve asked as they climbed.

"I don't want it leaking to Nathaniel Hoestler," Jake said simply. "You know Grant's here, but we snuck in and hopefully wouldn't otherwise appear on your radar until Monday when records of our flight were finally entered. We're playing a hunch that Nathaniel expects us to not arrive before mid-week."

"And the folks you ambushed here tonight?"

"You get at least two of them to take home with you," Jake said. "Spencer might have found a clue up in the apartment. If he did, you can have her as well."

The man was at least smart enough to not ask at this point, since Jake wasn't about to tell him.

They got to the door and entered. The prisoner left behind had been blindfolded but not gagged. Hollyanne was with him.

"This is one?" Steve asked.

"Yup," Hollyanne replied.

"I'm not telling you bastards anything," the man growled in a Midlands accent.

"You don't have to, sweetie," Hollyanne cooed at him like the soft Southern Belle she wasn't. "We've got all the evidence we need to put you in prison forever, if I don't miss my guess. And all your friends as well. Those two are down in the truck waiting their turn for the Black Maria police van. All you can do now is roll on them or hope none of them rats on you."

"This way," Jake touched Steve and led him to the bedroom.

"Oh, shit," Steve recoiled when he saw the lab.

Jake had to agree. A couple of bins of chemicals that could be turned into right nasty devices. A stack of burner cell phones that made excellent timers or remote detonators. Wires and boards and other things.

"They sleep in the other bedroom," Jake said. "Guy out front and the girl, near as I can tell. This was their workshop. Spencer?"

Spencer had been taking photos. Now, he pointed at a stack of books and papers to one side. Jake approached them gingerly, same as Spencer had, and examined the piece he needed. The stack felt random rather than a trap, but he still pulled the one page out slowly and looked at it.

Blueprints. Big building. Jake turned it over and pointed at the title.

One Chamberlain Square. Birmingham. Part of a massive downtown renovation to undo some of the ugliness of the '70s.

"And the girl is a Red?" Steve asked.

"Close enough," Jake agreed. "Mostly mercenary, according to the folks that twitched us onto her in the first place. Between rumors of bombs and someone finding Mikhail Ivanov in London at the same time, we presume Hoestler never left the country and has something big planned here instead."

"What?"

"We're hoping you could tell us," Jake replied.

"Me?"

"Birmingham nails down a where, but only in the sense that something would happen nearby but not that close," Jake explained. "Nathaniel and Pacific Force means that everyone should expect it to have happened by mid-week."

"How close?" Steve asked warily.

"Close enough that every cop and agent who could get there would swarm into the downtown area as soon as a bomb went off, but they'd be too late," Jake said. "Then when something else happened elsewhere, everyone would be trapped in Birmingham and unable to respond quickly enough to do anything."

"I keep forgetting how many times your team has thwarted Hoestler and his crew." Steven shook his head. "Is this a red herring?"

"Probably," Jake agreed now. "Even if you started pouring teams in, the chances are low that you'd have any luck. Her bomb is probably already in place somewhere around there. If you do put more than one team in place, you'll just be stepping on each other's toes."

"What do you want from me?" Steve ignored the rest of the room and turned to face Jake now.

"What government targets are within maybe fifty miles of downtown Birmingham?" Jake asked.

"Why government?"

"If he was hitting a toff for ransom, he wouldn't need a bomb," Jake explained. "This is something big enough that he wants your people hot and heavy elsewhere."

"Let me talk to my people," Steve offered now.

Jake recognized that this was likely to have to go to the Home Secretary or at least an extremely senior bureaucrat in an office somewhere before they could talk to Pacific Force.

"Good," Jake said. "Let's go down to the truck and you can collect all three of your prisoners."

"What about you?" Steve asked, surprised.

"We're leaving as soon as you call in all your strike teams," Jake laughed. "Grant will phone you in the morning and hopefully you'll have good news. If Nathaniel hears about all this, maybe he just thinks that someone else tumbled them and the authorities got a lucky tip. He'll twitch, but not enough to abandon his plans, and we can maybe catch him in the act."

"Seems risky," Steve said, as Jake led him out front and nodded to Hollyanne to get this prisoner up on his feet.

"Everything is a risk," Jake said. "Sometimes you've just got to roll the dice."

CHAPTER
NINETEEN

NATHANIEL WAS ENJOYING some Tanzanian Peaberry coffee this morning with a classical, full Irish breakfast when Lucky walked in, looking like the man who had drawn the short straw from the sheepishness on his face. Nathaniel wiped up some egg yolk with his bacon and studied his minion as the man came to rest on the far side of the dining room table.

Nathaniel wondered if that barrier was a psychological comfort, or maybe some sort of calculation that it would give a victim a head start. He didn't do violence, but all of his men had been broken to his will at some point. Most of them had been common thugs and hooligans, lacking direction for their violence and needing someone like him to provide it.

Lucky had proven his namesake many times, surviving circumstances that might have gotten others killed.

The man stood perfectly still now, a six foot four columnar apple tree in winter sleep. Nervous, though he was hiding it well. On the verge of flinching, but holding up.

Nathaniel finished this piece of bacon and sipped some more coffee before he spoke.

"What happened?" he asked simply.

"Someone raided the bombmaker overnight," Lucky said carefully, his Kenyan accent still there underneath the East End he'd picked up over the last fifteen years. "Took 'em down hard and fast. Reports of a small explosion, but outside in the street, rather than a breach or a secondary explosion inside."

"Tommy send you in to get abused for bad news?" Nathaniel queried.

Lucky shrugged, which was quite a sight starting at his knees and going all the way up to the way his afro was carved into a peaked fade that made him look eight feet tall.

"Not sure what it changes," Lucky replied. "Tommy figured you'd be pissed."

"Any news from our spies in The City?" Nathaniel pressed.

"Is Sunday, so they be at home," Lucky said. "If they have not been called, maybe good. Maybe bad."

"Reach out and confirm that," Nathaniel said. "Then contact the team in Birmingham and let them know to be extra careful and ready to abort if someone finds our package. Let it be disarmed without incident. Confirm that."

"Let the bomb be disarmed without incident if the cops find it." Lucky nodded. "What if they get there too late and is ready to boom? Do we keep eyes on all the way?"

"When we leave here at ten, you'll check in with them and confirm," Nathaniel ordered the man. "And again at dinner."

"Me?"

Lucky was surprised, but he'd always been something of a third wheel with Tommy and Mikhail around.

"You." Nathaniel smiled disarmingly. "Tommy expected you to have to deal with the blowup that was coming from me finding out. So deal with it."

Now, the beanpole smiled. Nodded even.

"Gotcha, boss," he said, looking already a foot taller from the slump that had hunched him some earlier. "Anything else?"

"Tell Tommy I'm super pissed and ripped you a new asshole." Nathaniel grinned after a moment. "And nobody should bother me for a while. Then set an alarm for 0930 to make sure everything is packed in the truck."

"On it." And he departed, leaving Nathaniel to finish his beans and last piece of toast in peace.

Tommy was being a shit. Probably angling to make himself something like Chief of Staff, with Mikhail gone and expecting Lucky to get a ration of shit right now. Eliminating all the competition at the trough, as it were.

Already, it had looked like time to expand the gang by bringing in some bigger players.

After this, Nathaniel really needed to hire some pros. Luckily, he'd make a king's ransom for tonight.

Who did he need to bring in, outside of the usual channels?

JAKE HAD WATCHED the morning news enough to confirm that everyone was all aflutter about the raid, but Steve hadn't told anyone anything of value, so hopefully Nathaniel hadn't spooked.

Assuming that Nathaniel was still in-country, still planning something, and all of this wasn't a triple cross of some sort to distract Jake and the others. The original clues had pointed to Nathaniel making it successfully to Spain and then vanishing, but that was easy to do when you have that much coastline to work with and so many quiet revolutionary elements floating around in the background of Iberian history.

Jake always wondered how long Spain would continue to be a place before it fragmented into somewhere between two and six pieces, undoing the original fifteenth century Conquest that had driven out the Moors and the Jews in the first place. ETA might have finally gone quietly, but there were other groups. Other demands.

The world was not getting more cohesive and peaceful, even with everything Pacific Force could do.

They had driven back to the Birmingham area, the

suburb known as Solihull on the southeast, to spend the night. Rik had driven and the rest had napped, then crashed when they got to the house. It was morning now. Late church, if you were all into that sort of thing, though Jake wasn't, and didn't care if any of the others did.

They were on a mission right now, so religion could wait until later.

Spencer had gotten up early and baked cinnamon rolls, then fried bacon once folks emerged, so they were all sitting around the dining room having coffee, noses generally buried in phones getting the latest news. Or lack thereof.

Grant had remained in London somewhere, so he looked central to an investigation that wasn't there anymore.

Jake's phone rang. Unknown number. Not an uncommon occurrence, but he was on an English phone, rather than his own number, so not many people would know how to get hold of him.

"Oy?" he answered, flattening his accent down to something more Yorkshire and maybe a little grumpy.

"Uhm, Jake?" Steve asked.

"That's right," Jake replied, shifting back to his normal tones. "What do we know this morning?"

"The Undersecretary would like to be briefed personally. By you and the team," Steve said carefully. "Today. In London. Well, Northampton. We've established something of a base of operations there that should be far enough away from Birmingham but within range. The Undersecretary is headed that way now."

Jake suppressed the sarcastic reply on the tip of his tongue. This was one of the reasons that Jake had never wanted to belong to any agency anywhere. The amount of bureaucratic red tape as everyone had to cover his or her ass against possibly making a mistake that could not be blamed on someone else meant that things moved at a glacial pace.

Normally, that was a good thing, as you wanted a government that moved with calm deliberation, but there were times like now when Nathaniel was no doubt counting on that sort of dithering.

And the English were famous for dithering.

Still, either the man had an Issue #1 he wanted signed by the team or knew something so utterly disturbing that it had to be communicated in person. Both had happened over the years.

"Two hours?" Jake asked. "Take us an hour to drive and a little time here to prep."

Steve covered the phone at his end enough to muffle the words, but not the sound. Probably sitting next to the man in the back of a blacked-out Suburban right now.

The discussion lasted longer than a simple question, but Jake held his temper.

Finally, the man returned. Too long.

"That will be acceptable," Steve said in a tone similar to that of a child called on to apologize to all the adults in the room for something.

He gave Jake the address and hung up once Jake confirmed it.

Jake dialed Grant, who picked it up immediately.

"Yo."

"Are you in the front seat of a vehicle containing Steve and a gentleman in a striped tie?" Jake asked simply.

"Affirmative."

"We'll see you then."

Jake hung up and finished his coffee before he decided to blister the reputation of all bureaucrats everywhere. At least they had grabbed Grant on their way out of town. Not exactly a hostage, but certainly a statement that Grant's investigation was over.

Not that Jake wouldn't have pulled the man north by lunch anyway, but this still felt a little like hostage taking and left a sour taste in Jake's mouth.

The others were all eyes when he carefully placed his empty coffee mug on the table, rather than slamming it hard enough that it might crack.

Much as he wanted to.

He drew a long, deep breath and released it. He turned and focused his attention on Rik.

"We'll be headed to Northampton shortly to meet with someone," he said in a flat, angry tone. "I suspect that said someone will want his hand held excessively today, to the extent that we will not be able to get into the field and conduct our own investigations in time to possibly have any impact on whatever happens. We'll need to arrange something extravagant in order to get us wherever we need to be in a minimum of time when all hell breaks loose while we're stuck babysitting."

Rik nodded placidly.

"How stupid do you want to get?" she asked.

"If the gentleman in question, the one about to drag us all in to demonstrate his political power, tells us anything useful, maybe not at all," Jake smiled.

"Right," Rik nodded. "Completely, fucking insane coming up. Do you care?"

"I do not," Jake assured her, watching all three of his friends flinch at the implications.

Usually, Jake set down limits and let everyone color inside those lines, but right now he was chewing nails angry at the hostage-taking element of things and didn't really care who knew.

"Actually, I do care," Jake countered after a moment. "Stupidly fast when I need to get somewhere."

"*Stupidly* fast?" Rik repeated delicately.

"*Stupidly*," Jake confirmed. "Everyone else, I propose we pack some snacks, and whatever gear you think you'll need physically on you at the moment that the idiot in Northampton decides that maybe we should have been in the field all day instead of holding his hand while he talked to someone in London anyway. Let's pack and then depart in forty-five minutes for the drive down. Questions?"

Everyone shook their heads, so Jake picked up his mug, put it in the sink, and headed to his room to grab a few things. Hollyanne had apparently followed him because she was standing in the door when he looked back.

"Are they going to try to burn us on this one?" she asked.

"I doubt that the gentleman in question has thought that far ahead," Jake replied primly. "If he's capable of that level of inductive logic. He's probably still slowly working his way down a checklist filled with people he can bully and browbeat because they work for him, civil service or not."

"And what will you do if he does piss you off?"

"You mean more?" Jake asked.

"Yes, more."

"I might call Whitehall and complain to the PM. Maybe leave a message at Buckingham, assuming she's not in Scotland right now," Jake said. "If he really pisses me off, we'll just fly back to Seattle tonight instead, and he can fucking deal with the problem himself."

"You said yourself that they couldn't handle Nathaniel, Jake," Hollyanne was almost pleading with him now.

"That was why we had to get back together and go into the field again."

"Indeed." Jake let his face curl into a snarl. "But they seem to think otherwise. I am currently tempted to let them deal with things, having broken it open enough that perhaps they feel they can handle this."

"Are you emotionally compromised?" she asked.

"No," Jake decided. "I'm angry. Not quite angry enough, but close."

She didn't ask what form that would take, which was good. Because if this fool blew it all and then decided that he'd want to blame the Americans for it anyway, Jake would make a point of getting the man so badly black-balled by his own government that he would end up manning a research station in Antarctica if he wanted the rest of his pension.

TWENTY-ONE

GRANT KEPT a low profile as the truck pulled into a warehouse and someone already inside closed the door behind them. Steve at least had the courtesy to look chagrined as everyone got out of the vehicle and followed the portly man in the striped suit and raspy wheeze over to an area that had been temporarily configured as a command post. Or somebody's idea of what one looked like, probably from some movie he watched.

There was a map covering the ring roads around Birmingham. Another showing the smaller downtown area that was being rebuilt. One with all of England, marked with obscure red symbols: crosses, circles, squares, starbursts.

Grant couldn't find a legend anywhere but supposed that he didn't rate that sort of security clearance with these people. He could have told them otherwise, but that had been several years ago and, he didn't know anyone in the present space except for Steve.

The Undersecretary made a production of checking his watch as he turned to spear Grant with the sort of hard eye the man probably usually reserved for the dessert cart.

"Where is he?" the Undersecretary demanded.

Grant pulled his phone out of his jacket pocket and checked the time. And to see if he had any voicemails or texts from anyone who might have remembered something or told a friend.

The web of connections he had was huge. Usually passive, but at a time like this he had thrummed it pretty hard in order to nail down a bombmaker in London with bad friends.

There were others out there.

"You told him seventeen minutes from now," Grant replied politely.

He already knew how pissed Jake was, just from the previous phone call. And for knowing the guy since they were fourteen.

"I expect better service," the Undersecretary huffed.

Steve happened to be standing beyond the man. Behind him in such a way that Grant and a few others could see the grimace of pain that flashed over the spy's face at those words.

But the Undersecretary didn't live in their world. He lived in a place where tea was predictable, and you could be assured of the proper dill pickle wedges perfectly chilled and possibly hand-dried before serving.

Grant hadn't even had time to get a pasty from the corner shop before Steve and friends had showed up for him this morning, but he wasn't going to say anything just yet.

If anything, he might need to play good cop with what was coming up.

Or not.

"Sir, we've identified their vehicle," a woman spoke up from a table that had been partly hidden by map stands. Army green jacket with her hair pulled back in a bun. Quite cute. "Inbound. ETA three minutes."

Grant just smiled politely, rather than suggest any sort of 'I told you so' with his body language.

There was a coffee urn close. One of those nasty, upright silver trash cans that held coffee long past the point that it was still viable. Grant ignored everyone and went for coffee. And donuts in a picked over box that was probably for the field techs.

Grant was certain that the Undersecretary's favorite biscuits were in an office somewhere nearby, along with a proper tea service. Possibly had a butler or a batman along supervising. Everyone else wandered off to whatever they were doing as the Undersecretary took a seat at the head of a conference table that had been installed.

Steve approached and grabbed a paper cup for his own coffee as Grant finished filling his.

"Sorry about all this," the man murmured under the sound of soldiers and folks being proactively busy with bosses around. "How's Jake?"

"How close to your pension are you?" Grant murmured back as he added powdered milk and sugar substances to adulterate his sludge. He smiled at the man.

"Ouch," Steve said with another wince.

"Is there any way of getting that twit off high-center before tomorrow?" Grant asked.

"I don't know," Steve offered. "I ran it up my food chain, and it got that far when the Permanent Undersecretary apparently decided that he was the man to take charge of the investigation."

"He got any experience with something like this?" Grant moved to one side and let Steve work.

The cute woman in green was across a table, glancing at him right now, but otherwise keeping up a steady chatter over a headset. She'd been the one that had announced Jake and the team.

Grant smiled at her.

"None," Steve answered. "I wonder if he thinks this catapults him into the upper reaches of the Ministry. Or even a knighthood."

"Anything is possible," Grant offered ambiguously.

Pacific Force was not a group that sat around warehouses briefing officious twits about how investigations were running. They had Steve's people for that sort of thing.

Grant should be running down leads in London and talking to people. Jake and the others should be getting into position to intercept Nathaniel and his hooligans as soon as any clue emerged from the fog.

Now, all of them were going to be spinning their wheels in a three-ring circus in Northampton.

Charming.

One of the garage doors opened and Rik blasted the Rover in, not quite side-skidding it to a stop next to the Suburban Grant had traveled north in, but close. Still showing off.

Grant stayed put here. Jake was in the front seat looking perfectly composed and elegant in such a way that suggested that *A)* butter might not melt in his mouth right now, and *B)* he might in a mood to verbally eviscerate someone and then piss on their corpse afterwards.

Steve took his cue from the way Grant was sitting on the edge of the work desk with his back to the woman and joined him. They were at least well away from the Undersecretary and the fireworks Grant could smell coming.

CHAPTER
TWENTY-TWO

HOLLYANNE MANAGED to bail out of the Rover before anyone else could. Moving quickly, she got into a position in case she needed to intercept things. Jake had fallen utterly silent for the last ten minutes of the drive, and Hollyanne knew how close he was to losing his temper.

Unfortunately, she couldn't think of anything that they might do at this point unless the Undersecretary decided to relax some of the information security he was sitting on and letting Pacific Force know more about the inner workings of the Department than normal.

Fool over there looked smug, like he was going to stonewall them. That much was obvious just from the way he was sitting. Demand that they sit around here at his beck and call until something happened and then try to blame them for not stopping it, regardless of the fact that he had demanded they wait on him.

She wondered how long until Jake called someone at the Palace and blew this entire situation into a billion pieces. She tried to smile at him, but the smile she got back was brittle and angry.

The Undersecretary was seated at a conference table. Hollyanne fell in next to Jake and walked over. Grant and his contact were over yonder, watching. Rik and Spencer had gotten out of the Rover, but not gotten any closer, leaning against the nearest front fender, both with hands in pockets.

Around them, half the staff were technical agents, on the phone, on the comm, or moving paper around and updating boards. The other half were the field teams, dressed in the sorts of gray camouflage that worked well in a city at night. There were guns, but they were all racked for now over against a wall for need.

She got more than one half-smile from the soldiers, but most of them probably knew her on sight. She only recognized a few from previous operations, but Pacific Force had hung it up two years ago when Nathaniel was captured the first time.

Jake was not going to make the obvious play and sit at the far end of the table, directly across from the tall, fat man in the expensive, silk suit, so Hollyanne did. Technically, last night had been her operation, and she was Jake's Second-in-Command most of the time anyway.

She sat and faced the man. Jake was closer to her end than his.

Hollyanne composed herself and rested her forearms on the table, looking at the man down there. Fifty, perhaps. Badly aged, like milk left out. The suit should have been retailored again, as he'd put on a stone or so since the last time it had been let out. Special tie, related to some organization he belonged to. An American politician would be wearing a fraternity tie to cover the same ground.

Hollyanne was in her favorite *gi* pants. Faded from black to a charcoal, and the elastic around her ankles was old enough that she'd probably have to replace it again soon. White T-shirt tucked in over a sports bra made with enough Kevlar to turn a knife in close. She'd left the rest of the *gi* at the house and worn a blue, denim jacket she'd originally bought in Aberdeen a few years ago.

Jake was in newer blue jeans. Buttoned-down Archer shirt she'd gotten him for Christmas, medium blue with thin red stripes. Charcoal trench coat, also lined with Kevlar, but warm against wind and rain, and lots of pockets inside and out.

Casual, in face of official.

The Undersecretary wore steel-blue wool. Single-breasted with two buttons and medium lapels. But the government these days was Tory, so that was not out of the ordinary. Stark white shirt. That ugly tie that was going to become the man's entire shorthand description, one of these days.

Hollyanne refrained from checking the shoes the man wore. She and Jake both wore dark three-quarter-tops, designed for running, jumping, and kicking, as well as with soles that would stop a nail and aluminum toes. Not as good as steel. Not as heavy, either.

Grant looked a question her way, but Hollyanne shook her head. Let him stay over there, just like Spencer and Rik were staying by the truck. This was going to be a clash of the titans over here. The Undersecretary was already stewing. Jake was stewing.

But this was her op, so fuck you people.

She considered letting things build to a head by out-waiting the man, but decided that doing that would endgame things badly.

"What have you learned from the prisoners we turned over to you last night?" she asked in a bright and innocent voice.

Not only accusing them of having all the cards, but perhaps reminding them as well.

The Undersecretary blinked. Blinked a second time.

Not the game he'd been expecting, perhaps? Or perhaps he was English, and she was a Persian-American woman, technically a princess, depending on who you asked and how you framed the question.

Short, dark, and feminine. But then, the PM was female these days. And a Tory.

Not that Hollyanne would accuse the English of a tendency towards polite racism. If anything, they were more classist than racist, though she could look down on a *mere civil servant* from a dizzying height if he wanted to go there with her, too.

She settled for a smile.

"I was expecting you to brief my team about the terrorist," the man finally huffed.

"Which one?" Hollyanne asked.

"What do you mean, which one?" the Undersecretary demanded.

"We captured a mercenary bombmaker, an assistant or boyfriend, and perhaps a complete stranger who just happened to be dropping in for a spot of tea," Hollyanne continued, still smiling. "We turned them over to your team for interrogation more than twelve hours ago and left. You demanded that we attend you here in Northampton rather than continuing our own investigations into things. At present, we have a theory that your intelligence assessment is wrong, and that Nathaniel Hoestler never left this island. However, we have no proof and are not in a position to investigate any of the leads we have worked up. At present, we expect you to provide that information, one way or the other."

Hollyanne leaned back now, aware that she had braced her feet under the table as if she needed to flow immediately into combat. The table was too heavy to throw, although Jake might be angry enough right now to flip it, but she could always jump up on it and run the length in a hurry if she had to.

She smiled to convey that to the man down there. Someone off to one side snickered so quietly that it would have been missed, had the entire space not dropped to the silence of a tomb.

The Undersecretary flushed, but she couldn't tell if that was embarrassment at being called out, or rage for the same. Either way, she hadn't voted for the current government, and didn't pay any taxes to support it.

They could ask her to help. Politely.

Jake took this moment to lean his chair back, roll it a few inches backwards, and literally kick his feet up on the table like a man behind a desk, crossing them at the ankles.

Hollyanne wasn't sure you could more perfectly insult a Permanent Undersecretary to his face.

She wasn't fooled by Jake's supposed insouciance, or the carefree way his hands were laced behind his head. He was as keyed up for potential violence as she was, but his was entirely political.

"Now you see here, young lady…" the fat man started to bellow, but she turned to Jake and ignored the diatribe starting to roll down there.

"Sushi or curry for lunch?" she asked in a quiet enough voice that only someone reading her lips could tell.

Back home, they'd get Chinese take-out or a couple of pizzas delivered, but this was the English Midlands. Totally different culture separated by a language called English in both places.

The Undersecretary ran out of steam like a pricked balloon when he realized that the only people looking at him were the ones in his employ.

Hollyanne gave him a look like a Headmistress with a tardy child. Then she ignored him and looked around at the civilians and soldiers around her. Anyone not wearing Army green in here was some sort of spy.

A clock on the wall read 1:07 pm.

"Did anyone actually interrogate the prisoners?" Hollyanne asked the room. "Or just threaten them enough to shut them up without telling you anything?"

Several faces fell and nobody would make eye contact with her at that point, not even Grant's primary contact.

She turned back to the Undersecretary and scowled at him. Watched the man shrink just a little from the animated bellicosity that he had been all set to pursue earlier.

"We're here because you demanded it," she announced, in a voice verging on suggesting that the man was an idiot without—quite—painting him all the way into that corner. "This is now your operation. What will it be?"

Under all that bluster, the man finally seemed to come to understand that he was a peon, as far as she and Jake were concerned, but he'd done that to himself, demanding instead of asking. Northampton instead of Solihull.

Lots of little things.

"You people are the experts on Hoestler," he finally managed in a more restrained voice. "Nobody in my department knows him like you do."

"Nobody on this planet knows him like she and I do," Jake spoke for the first time in almost half an hour. "I will presume, looking around the room, that you either didn't choose to bring the experts you did have on staff, or didn't bother asking after the folks that helped us capture him the first time. There is only one face here I recognize here, the gentleman over there using the cover name *Steve*."

Hollyanne nodded to herself and leaned back.

Jake looked ready to own the game board finally.

Maybe without setting it on fire first.

JAKE CONSIDERED KEEPING his feet up on the table like a rude teenager. That sort of insult transcended oceans, even if the target of his ire was probably clueless about such things. But the Undersecretary represented the past.

Pacific Force was, in many ways, the future, if only because Jake doubted that the UK government was any less corrupt than anywhere else. Money and power. They just dressed in fancier attire than some of the places he'd been.

Everywhere he had looked, money and power had formed oligopolies intent on retaining control. In the democratic nations, they paid lip service to swapping parties on a regular basis, and in doing so usually managed to advance civilization haltingly.

But you still needed free agents with money, willing to put themselves and their fortunes on the line, to really make the world a better place.

This Permanent Undersecretary was apparently the sort of fool who had started believing his own press releases.

"Yes," Jake continued into that vast, hollow silence

that had fallen. "We know Nathaniel Hoestler better than anyone, because the five of us went to private school with the man, twenty years and more ago. We've fought him any number of times, mostly stopping his little games without ransoms being paid or hostages getting hurt, because he does play by a set of hard and fast rules, however odd you might interpret them."

Jake rose from the chair and rolled it under the table as a mechanism to keep himself from getting angry.

Angrier.

Idiot fops in expensive ties, making power plays they didn't understand.

How badly did he wish to burn the British government today? Jake wasn't sure. But he'd never been treated like a *servant* by them before, either.

"We presume Nathaniel is involved, without any concrete evidence," Jake said. "Mikhail Ivanov was one of his inner circle, and the man was beaten, killed, and dumped in Battersea without any follow up or crowing, like you might expect if Hoestler's enemies had done it. Then a bombmaker started working, at a time when most of those folks had been quietly negotiated into an abeyance of their craft. Being left alone for behaving, as it were. She's your prisoner. We suspect that a bomb was set to be exploded in Birmingham's core, but don't know when. Have you blown that operation apart by putting fifty men and women, uniformed and undercover, into the area?"

He'd been pacing as he spoke. Now, he found himself just behind Hollyanne, so he put a hand on the back of her chair and rested there for a moment, like a raptor waiting for the mouse to flush from cover.

The Undersecretary turned to Steve now and nodded the man to the table so hard he might have pulled something. At least Steve was a professional.

That spy detached himself from the table where Grant was and approached the center of things.

"We have one team on the ground, and a sniper team in a discrete spot for oversight," Steve explained.

"So you've probably been seen," Jake replied, letting his voice come down to conversational instead of confrontational. For a while.

Steve shrugged.

"That will possibly be evident only in retrospect," he said. "For now, we have sufficient teams on call but around the edges of the city, plus this command post."

"What do you have within fifty miles of One Chamberlain Square that might be a good primary target for Hoestler to hit?" Jake asked.

"Quite a number of facilities," Steve replied carefully. "We have raised the alert status on several of them and had them bring in security patrols on their perimeters. If anyone attempts an attack, they will be prepared."

"Nathaniel is not a terrorist," Jake said.

"The devil you say, McNeil," the Undersecretary slammed a hand angrily onto the table. "Hostage taking, bomb planting, assassinations. This man Hoestler is very much a terrorist and you had better begin thinking of him as such if you wish to remain part of this investigation."

Jake closed his mouth on the theory that words unsaid right now wouldn't have to be repeated in front of the Minister himself at a later date. Or an Ambassador. Or anybody important at the Palace.

Jake chose to simply ignore the outburst for now, rather than rising to the bait like a shark intent on tearing a hunk out of a swimmer. Much as he wanted to.

Oh, so much as he wanted to.

"Let us, for the sake of discussion, assume that Nathaniel has an operation in mind," Jake offered to Steve.

"He needs the authorities off-balance and removed from some location for a set period of time while he runs his op. Given the ubiquity of cellular phones, it will be a secured facility where nobody is allowed personal communications devices, probably one with an extremely small staff. Low profile, so he can get close, hit the place, and fade before anyone can react."

"That does not narrow things down now, does it?" the Undersecretary replied, verging back over to his earlier bellicosity.

Jake again chose to ignore him, speaking for the crowd of soldiers and field officers around him, in the hopes that one of them might risk his or her career by speaking up right now.

"Nathaniel has always used a team of professional killers for things," Jake continued. "Men who have been with him for years, know how to handle a gun, and when to rely on fists instead. Intimidation instead of bloodshed, which was why nobody ever put a significant-enough bounty on his head to bring him in."

"Until you mercenaries decided to get involved," the Undersecretary sniped.

"Mercenaries?" Jake rounded on the man again. He'd been pacing and was midway up the left now. "After our expenses, which weren't much, the rest of the reward money for Nathaniel's capture went to the JM Barrie fund. Children's Hospitals, I believe is what they finance. We itemized our expenses, and they came in around roughly fifteen thousand pounds. What was Nathaniel worth that day?"

The last he fired at Grant, enough behind the Undersecretary to have that fuck-wit slightly surrounded, and maybe give him a small case of whiplash.

"Quarter of a million pounds," Grant said simply.

Jake nodded and zeroed in hard on the Undersecretary

"That's as much as I can tell you, without a better idea of where he's going after," Jake said flatly.

He returned to that first chair and sat.

"What do you need to know?" Steve asked, still standing and almost directly across the table from Jake now.

"Fifty-mile radius," Jake said. "Facilities by location, purpose, and importance."

"You are not cleared for that information," the Undersecretary interrupted aggressively, again slapping his hand on the table.

That sort of thing probably worked with other civil servants he could bully. Jake just found it annoying and counter-productive.

"Not cleared?" he confirmed in a slow, almost mocking tone just this side of a sarcasm even an Englishman would appreciate.

The Undersecretary assumed an evil smile now.

"That is correct," he intoned in a haughty, superior tone. "You people are civilian mercenaries and American. You are not even members of Her Majesty's Forces."

Jake considered things for a long moment. He nodded enthusiastically and turned to Hollyanne.

"He's right, you know," Jake said.

Her face had gone cold and still, so she understood what was coming. Just watching him for a cue.

Jake turned to the Undersecretary as he rose.

"I don't believe that there is anything else we can do at this point," Jake announced in a much brighter, breezier tone. "We've told you what we know. Hopefully, it will be sufficient. With that, we shall depart and return to Seattle. Good day."

Rik was already moving before Spencer and Grant

woke up and started walking. Hollyanne was out of her chair and in stride.

"What do you think you are doing?" the Undersecretary demanded loudly.

"Leaving," Jake said distinctly. "This is, as you have said, your investigation. We are not privy to anything that might allow us to contribute. Best of luck."

"I will not allow it!" the man thundered.

"That is entirely your choice." Jake's anger suffused him now. "Perhaps I should call Sir William at the Palace and ask him for an official opinion on your interpretation of the matter?"

If putting your feet up on a table was an insult, those words conveyed a level of deadly threat that sliced neatly through the fat man's anger, real or not. Sir William might just have someone like the Permanent Undersecretary blackballed so brutally that taking an early retirement and getting a job tending bar for a publican in Inverness might be all he had left open to him.

Jake ignored the man now and whatever he wanted to say after that. Anything after this would begin with a formal apology and then get serious. Perhaps personal.

Jake was done.

He got into the Rover and leaned an arm and head out to literally snap his fingers at the men guarding the big door as Rik got the green beast in gear and began a sharp U-turn inside the garage, all five of them crammed in for now.

The sergeant glanced back at the main part of the group, got whatever approval he thought he needed, and let rip on the chain, opening it quickly.

The Rover emerged into mid-day gloom, and Rik floored it across the parking lot.

"Now what?" Grant asked after a few moments.

"Now, they get to decide how badly they want our help." Hollyanne spoke before Jake could, but only to say the same thing with fewer sharp edges. "You'll return with us to Solihull for now and maybe call some of your friends in London for updates, but we need to remain together. We can make arrangements for your other gear if we have to."

"Should I update our transportation reservations for five?" Rik asked. "Just in case?"

"Yes," Jake decided aloud. "I have a feeling that whatever they have planned is going to happen tonight. The bombmaker thought things were imminent when she sent her stuff on yesterday. Monday will be too busy for a good getaway."

"We still gonna stop him? Rik asked.

"That's no longer our call," Jake said.

Then he lapsed into silence.

NATHANIEL WAS HAVING a bit of tea and something of a…well, not a nap, because he wasn't asleep, so much as meditating quietly. He'd had to do that quite a bit in prison, focusing on quietness so that he didn't give in and start ranting.

He hadn't been the largest of the prisoners, nor the smallest. Perhaps among the highest profile within certain niche audiences.

Meditating was something he had learned to keep his sanity intact.

A knock at the door brought him fully to the surface of his mind. He was resting on a bed, seated upright against the headboard.

They were staying in a house that had been rented by an agency without ever meeting anyone in person. Just a credit rating, a credit card, and planning. Nathaniel had any number of perfectly serviceable identities he could use, the products of burrowing deep into the bowels of the internet in the very early days, when the Dark Web was still a wild west sort of place.

These days, at least every other person you were likely to find in such searches belonged to a government agency of some sort, and those tended to be much harder to subvert. Not impossible, mind you. Just a higher price.

The door opened and Lucky stuck his head in far enough to make eye contact. Nathaniel nodded and the man slipped in, closing the door behind him.

"Bit of a ruckus in Birmingham, sir," he said without preamble. "You told me to pay attention, so I let the team know to be extra cautious."

Nathaniel nodded. Lucky earning his stripes, as it were.

"What did they see?"

"Sniper team," Lucky said with a shudder. "Close enough to our target zone that they aren't random chance, but no significant build-up of forces otherwise."

"What's happening in London?" Nathaniel asked.

He had considered whether or not this mission needed to be scrubbed when the authorities got his bombmaker last night, but he couldn't imagine that she'd have cracked so quickly. Must have left some sort of clue lying about and someone had guessed right.

If Jake was here, that was the sort of thing he routinely did, but he'd sent Grant ahead to scour London, never thinking to look up-country so quickly.

Because, truth be told, Nathaniel needed the money. Running a criminal enterprise like this required constant cash flow. Staff to maintain. Safe houses to keep. Bribes to pay.

Some days, he wondered if going straight would be less of a pain in the ass. A few early internet phreakers had paid their debts to society and then went about earning a living as security experts. 'Captain Crunch' was just one of the more famous.

Lucky was shifting his weight back and forth uncomfortably. Nathaniel's face hardened.

"Can't tell, sir," the man said in his East End/East African sing-song. "Some of our contacts have gone missing today when we might have expected them to be at the pub or answering the phone. Others report a spot of busyness in places that should be slumbrous on a Sunday."

Nathaniel was always a bit taken sideways when Lucky used such complicated language, but that innocent face concealed a great deal more formal education than was normal for the gang of hooligans Nathaniel had built and acquired.

"How so?"

"Lots of traffic inbound to certain ministry buildings we pay people to observe," Lucky suggested. "On a Sunday. Normally, that suggests a major crisis requiring top players be consulted and make official rulings. You know, Whitehall and them folk peeing all over things so the scent is right."

Nathaniel had to smile. Even with a woman in charge, not much had changed at the ranks below.

"On th'other hand, not much movement in the security folks what would be called upon if they were about to pop out of the woodwork," Lucky continued. "Mayhap folks is already in place 'round Birmingham-way. Mayhap nobody knows better, but you specifically wanted a call at this time of day about whether we should scrub things and walk."

Nathaniel nodded. He had. You always included a number of No/Go breakpoints in the plan, where it was necessary to determine if proceeding was a mistake.

Nothing had risen to that level so far. Grant Collingwood was in London, but that was part of Nathaniel's plan, and would keep everyone's focus south instead of north. Jake wouldn't show up until Wednesday or so. Maybe sooner if Grant was in contact with the folks who had disappeared his bombmaker, but he'd still need a day in transit from Seattle. Longer if the others decided to come as well.

Time. He just needed twelve more hours and he'd be gone. Better, they'd never expect the way he was leaving, and he'd slip right through their net even if they did react in time.

"Anything stand out to you, Lucky?" Nathaniel asked now.

"No, sir," the man hemmed a little. "Tight, but ya gotta almost be on top of us to intercept things, and we'd see that coming."

"I agree," Nathaniel decided. "Check in with both teams one last time and then we'll go to radio silence if they haven't seen any reason to stop."

"On it."

Nathaniel was alone again. Not unusual. Most of his team were poorly educated career criminals more at home at a pub with the telly tuned to a Premier match than to planning or accounting. Even Lucky was just better educated.

Nathaniel had no one with whom to share any portion of the burden of command and strategic operations. Not that he'd trust a spouse, but perhaps he needed a partner?

Where in the world did you find such a thing in this industry, though?

Certainly, something he'd need to consider, but not until Tuesday.

Right now, he needed to embarrass the British government yet again, draw a ransom with his right hand while selling his hostage with his left for a double payment, and then vanish into the night.

Maybe he needed to poke Jake next month, just to finally win one against the man. It had been twenty years stewing.

HOLLYANNE WAS IN THE KITCHEN. Normally, she'd putter and maybe make cookies or something, just to have something to do and to dissipate the mad energy that had accumulated, but she wasn't home and hadn't felt like stopping at a market for the things missing from the rental.

They'd gotten curry instead and eaten. Spencer and Grant were busy doing their own forms of research, Grant on the back porch on the phone and Spencer in his bedroom, diving headlong into the electronic pathways of the world.

Jake had retired to the living room and was reading, last she looked.

Rik wandered in and sat at the small table.

"How stupid is the fat guy in the tie?" she asked right off the bat.

"Highly educated," Hollyanne replied. "Excellent private schools. Eton and Oxford, but I'm not sure which college."

She paused there as Rik smiled.

"No, he probably has never met anything like Jake,"

Hollyanne continued. "Nor will he know what to do when his bluff has been called like that. Zero street smarts outside the ivory towers and marble halls."

"They got any leverage on us they might use?" Rik perked up.

"Not off the top of my head," Hollyanne decided. "They might send someone around to pick us up and haul us back to Northampton, but that would really piss Jake off, and the fat man's head on a chopping block is probably the dead minimum Jake would demand for ever again taking another phone call from the government or the Palace. I suspect that several people are having a number of quiet conversations around the country right now."

Rik nodded.

"Bear traps are ugly things," she said. "Especially the ones marked Bear Trap in big neon letters. How soon until the boss accepts an apology or decides to blow town?"

Hollyanne paused on that one. That was the rub. Jake had been absolutely correct that Pacific Force, at the end of the day, were private vigilante mercenaries that worked for reward money.

But they required the assistance of the governments they worked with. If that was withdrawn, there were any number of ways that the same government might throw roadblocks in the way.

Of course, if those same governments could do these things themselves, they wouldn't have needed Pacific Force in the first place. The US and UK had both—along with several others more quietly—militarized their responses to a number of issues and mostly done away with soft diplomacy over the last generation. Didn't matter which party, both had decided that it was simply easier to bomb people than bothering to talk to them.

"How soon?" Hollyanne repeated as a way to gain a

few seconds. "I don't know. Someone really stuck his dick in this one, and I don't think Jake's willing to offer him an out that isn't painful."

"Yeah," Rik said, rising suddenly. "Think I'll go call the airport and ask them to standby on prepping the jet for a return flight. Pilot's holed up at a nearby joint, but he knows us, so he's sober enough to fly if we need. Or I could take command and get us in the air well enough for the autopilot to take over. Then he's sobering up quickly enough."

"When did you get multi-engine jet certified?" Hollyanne asked, shocked.

But then, she hadn't spent that much time just with Rik in the last two years. With any of the boys, sure, but they had both been self-contained women, and neither of them did much socially. Only in the framework of Jake or Pacific Force.

Hollyanne decided that she needed to do something about that going forward.

"Last year." Rik smiled as she made it to the door. "Needed something to do that got me out of Jake's garage and hunting east of the mountains. Got enough friends and contacts that own jets that I could borrow for flight time to do it, just never wanted to own one. Too expensive a hobby, you know?"

"Says the woman who rebuilds cars and trucks constantly," Hollyanne replied with a laugh.

"Still Jake's money," Rik laughed with her. "Or Pacific Force's, which is the same thing. Let someone else spend theirs."

"You never spend any of yours?" Hollyanne asked, a little surprised.

"Hardly any, no." Rik was in the doorway now. "Got a job that pays reasonably and includes room and board, so it's not like I need much. And I make as much of my gear as I might buy, so its raw materials and time mostly."

"Huh," Hollyanne said. "Good to know. There were a few times over the last couple of years where renting a jet and having a friend who could fly it would have saved me some grief. Might see if you want to take a girl's vacation sometime."

"I look horrible in a bikini."

"Lies," Hollyanne laughed. "You make great bikini bait when we need a buxom blonde to distract people. I've seen it."

She watched the woman blush furiously now, but Rik didn't argue. Hollyanne wouldn't have given her an inch, anyway.

She just wasn't into girls, and Rik didn't like boys. But past that, Rik was just another one of the guys at the end of the day. Another big brother she'd known for twenty-odd years.

Rik slipped out and Hollyanne decided that it was her job now to go find Jake and see what the man had planned next.

She looked at the clock. 6:19 pm. The shadows were getting long, and she had to agree with everyone else's whispered beliefs that somewhere, a real bomb was ticking.

CHAPTER
TWENTY-SIX

JAKE LOOKED up as Hollyanne drifted into the living room. The others had all made a point of being elsewhere once they finished dinner, Hollyanne included, but he supposed that it was time to talk.

"Any messages?" he asked as she slipped onto the couch at the end closer to the comfortable chair he'd been meditating in.

"I'm sure Spencer and Grant have both been setting people and wires on fire, but nothing has made it as far as me," Hollyanne responded. "I assume you turned off your ringer. I just sent Rik to put our pilot on sixty-minute notice, in case we needed to depart tonight with little warning."

"Think I'm going to bail?" he asked her, watching the woman's body language.

Uncertain, but not negative. Not yet, anyway. They were a long way from being done with Nathaniel.

"I think the very act of filing a flight plan with the authorities will cause a lot of people indigestion over their Sunday dinner and glasses of port, regardless." Hollyanne smiled now. "What I don't know is how angry you are.

How willing to burn bridges here, or just burn everything down to prove a point. The old Jake wasn't like that, but we were twenty-something then. Forty's coming soon enough and we're probably going to start acting like grown-ups one of these days. Or supposed to, anyway."

"Supposed to," he agreed. Because she was right.

International crime fighter was a job for the young, but they were still active and capable. And nobody could take on Nathaniel as well as they could.

"Are we bluffing?" Hollyanne pressed.

"I am not bluffing," Jake said distinctly. "But that's not the same as acting. I haven't called Sir William or anyone else. Steve hasn't called me, and nobody else would get through because I don't have most of them programmed, so they can go to voicemail hell with all the rest of the telemarketers."

"Anyone offering bounties to go after telemarketing call center owners?" Hollyanne asked. "It feels like that would be the sort of place where we could really strike a blow for humanity and civilization."

"All the cell phone companies know who those folks are," Jake reminded her. "They could shut them down in ten seconds if they really wanted to. I presume they charge those folks an extra hefty amount to allow those calls to go through. Geese and golden eggs, as it were."

Hollyanne nodded.

"Still, might be fun," she said. "Pull the fire alarms to empty the building out and then go ahead and torch the place. No jury would ever convict once they knew who the target was."

Jake laughed. It felt good to relax. He'd been on edge since some pissant bureaucrat had ordered him and the team to call upon the man like a feudal lord.

Granted, England was closer to those roots than

America, but that was a level of bullshit he wasn't about to stand for.

"At this point, they've had five hours to marinate," Jake said. "We spent an hour and a half just getting home and eating, so we could roll at any time. But I'm sure someone had to call the Minister. Possibly more than one, plus several other people. Didn't expect anyone to have an answer much before now."

"What are we doing?" Hollyanne asked in a more serious tone.

"I never retired," Jake reminded her. "The other four of you took a long vacation, well deserved, but I talked you into coming back to the game. Maybe that was a mistake. Maybe not. I couldn't have imagined we'd get this sort of treatment, after the way we left things, but times change. People change. We have a new Permanent Undersecretary these days."

"Are you emotionally compromised?" Hollyanne probed now.

"Absolutely," Jake agreed. "What do you recommend we do?"

"Pack," she said simply. "Move everything and everyone to the airport. Do it right now. Put our gear on the plane. If we do need to do something tonight, Rik's backup plan is close at hand as well, so we save the time spent getting there. I agree with you that we can honestly say we tried at this point, even going so far are to capture the one lead that they probably needed to break the case. If they don't want our help, we don't foist ourselves off on them and instead go home."

"What about Monday?" he asked her, wondering at this new side of the woman.

Two years ago, Hollyanne Kadjar wouldn't have been

so ruthless. She was the philosopher of the team, not the hothead. That would be him, if anyone.

"You were working with Perkins last week, right?" she asked now.

Jake nodded.

"And I presume that if the whole team got back into the act, the Feds would be more polite and friendly." She smiled grimly. "Probably ecstatic. Plus, the Japanese and maybe even the Chinese at this point. We'll have options, even if we decide to never set foot in the United Kingdom again. Thoughts?"

"I like it," Jake decided. "Let's do it."

"You go pack," she said, rising. "I'll tell the others and we'll get in motion."

Jake followed her as far as the hallway and then split off.

He'd never retired, even when the rest had, so today had surprised him. The Brits had never done anything like this in the past. But if they didn't want his help, so be it.

Pacific Force had other fish they could fry. Monday might be a whole new world.

GRANT HAD his phone plugged into the wall charger after running it so nearly constantly today that it had gotten down to about a five percent charge at one point. London was stirred up pretty harshly, but nobody knew anything useful at this point. The bombmaker might have been the only fungible clue to be had this week. Texts had come in, but most of them didn't amount to anything helpful.

Just random static.

They were in the hangar's waiting area next to where the jet had been stored, a private space with lots of lighting and currently open to the sunset. The pilot who had come with the plane was still at his hotel, probably watching the telly, but could be here in fifteen minutes tops, so they were covered if Jake decided to actually walk away.

Grant had a pretty good view of the tarmac and saw a pair of headlights come around the main terminal building. He couldn't say what it was about them that got his attention, but they did. Late model sedan. Driving sedately. Maybe it was just the time of day, just as the night sky finally turned black.

He rose from his chair and whistled two notes just loud enough that the others looked over.

Jake and Hollyanne had been sitting with their heads together talking quietly, going over a map. Spencer was walking the web on the wi-fi, probably doing the same things Grant had, but with online folks. Rik had been doing something that smacked of dangerous rednecking with some metal tools and a few arrows, but he didn't ask.

There were some things you were better off not knowing…

After a moment, it was clear that the sedan was definitely heading their way. The rest of the team rose as well. Nobody had a gun, as far as Grant knew, but Rik had her bow, and the others were dangerous enough in case this was Nathaniel, having somehow figured out that they were all here and coming.

Except that he would have brought an entire team. Or maybe not. Maybe a couple of punks with machine guns. You never knew.

The sedan rolled to a polite stop outside the hangar, parked next to the Rover. Two doors opened and closed, but the figures were just shadows. Grant grabbed his phone and stuffed the charger into his pocket, just in case he needed to move.

England had gone weird.

Steve emerged into the light, alone, so the other guy was probably standing next to the car for now.

The man took in the situation and walked deliberately towards Grant, as if the others were invisible. He stopped about four feet away with a pained smile on his face.

"We looked for you at the house, but obviously you had already left," Steve said ambiguously.

"That's right," Grant replied, also ignoring everyone else, even though nobody was more than fifteen feet away right now. "We decided that we most likely wouldn't need a long-term rental on the house after all, as it looked like we might be departing tonight and returning to Seattle."

He left that hanging out there. Jake hadn't said anything about being contacted by someone that might convince the man otherwise. Not that there were all that many people in that category. Most of the contacts were through Grant anyway.

Steve grimaced like he'd been punched in the gut. Grant felt like commiserating, but not that much. Plus, Jake might be pissed enough to really punch the man.

"So there have been some developments since last we talked," Steve began circuitously. "The Permanent Undersecretary has been instructed to return to London to brief both the Secretary and the Minister. He left about ninety minutes ago, and we don't expect that he'll be back north tonight. Or possibly tomorrow, either."

"Pity," Grant offered in a brutal way. Still, that was still better than any of the others might have suggested. "Where's that leave you?"

Again, the grimace, thought this looked more like a man stepping out onto a ledge in a high, swirling wind.

"The Undersecretary did not bring any senior assistants with him," Steve said carefully. "When he was recalled, I suppose that left me as the senior civilian in the room, not that it counts for much, but the Army folks had their orders and weren't about to do anything without cover."

Grant could see that. A military fuckup of that degree could get you court-martialed in disgrace. Spies would just be fired, but their pension would remain intact, barring acts of treason or serious crimes.

"And?" Grant prompted, unwilling to cede the man even an inch at this point without more information.

"And I got a direct call from Sir William a few minutes

after the Undersecretary left," Steve said, loud enough that the others could hear him cleanly. "*Sub rosa*, as it were. Threats of being disowned if I told anyone else, but you needed to know and he understood that. I suspect that a Brigadier somewhere was being leaned on politely, if you catch my drift."

"Gotcha," Grant said. "Where's that leave everything?"

"I grabbed a few things from the command center in Northampton before I left for dinner," Steve said. "George has them in the boot outside. Didn't figure it was worth hauling much in the way of gear or people here and trying to convince you to come down guaranteed that we'd all be out of position when things went wrong."

"Have George join us," Jake ordered abruptly, stepping close.

Grant turned to Jake as Steve nodded and departed at a jog. This lounge had a couple of tables tucked into a corner, probably for a buffet event. He nodded to Rik as she rose, and they started grabbing them as Spencer and Hollyanne moved chairs around.

Steve returned quickly with several rolls of paper and a couple of tripods. He looked at the layout, and he and George moved to start setting things up.

"Rik, guessing we'll shortly need our other transport, after all," Jake announced. "Call him and let him know."

"On it," she replied.

Grant thought it was the craziest thing they'd ever done, but then corrected himself. Probably only made the top five, considering.

A polite, five-minute whirlwind left the space trans-formed. Three of the tripods were deployed, mapping Birmingham, including this very airport; a radius of one hundred miles like an atomic-bomb blast scale; and all of England.

"Do we care about the bomb at One Chamberlain Place?" Steve asked, standing opposite Hollyanne next to Jake.

"Only as the starting gun," Jake said. "Nathaniel has never been about gratuitous violence or property damage, and I can't see him starting now. If I'm wrong, I'll own that personally later with the Palace and Whitehall."

"As long as you're willing to do that," Steve said. "Rubs me wrong to just let someone set off a bomb and ignore him."

"If we tried to flood downtown Birmingham with teams, they wouldn't accomplish anything," Jake said. "At best, we find the bomb and maybe get it disarmed in time. You've still isolated all your forces in a tiny downtown area where they can't move quickly."

"Sunday night," Hollyanne mused. "Rik, what's the local forecast?"

"Cool but dry," Grant heard the tall woman reply instantly. "Broken clouds at thirty-five hundred meters and up. We had a few showers here and there mid-day, but that's all off over Lincolnshire and the North Sea by now. Probably pretty tomorrow."

"What are you thinking?" Grant asked the woman. "Who do I need to call?"

His phone was back on the charger, for what it was worth.

Her eyes got a faraway look to them.

"Jake, are we better off flooding Birmingham anyway?" she asked.

"Talk to me."

"So, if Nathaniel wants all the local cops and agents out of his way, do we get them out of our way as well?" she asked. "Give him the game board he originally planned for?"

"Might not be a bad idea," Jake agreed.

Everyone froze when Steve's cell rang. He studied it, swallowed heavily, and answered.

"Go ahead," he said, but his face fell, and all the blood drained out it as he listened for several seconds. "Okay, roll all contingencies as the Undersecretary had planned them."

He hung up and looked around.

"We're too late," he said simply. "The bomb just went off in Birmingham. Small one, from the initial report. Briefcase, maybe, like we expected. Loud, but does not appear deadly at this time."

"What were your contingencies?" Grant asked.

"What we were discussing," Steve said. "All the normal outfits and teams respond as they would to any terrorist event, despite us knowing ahead of time."

"What's Northampton doing?" Jake asked.

"Waiting for orders."

TWENTY-EIGHT

JAKE GRIMACED, but it was out of his hands. The bomb had not been found in time. Hopefully nobody had been killed just now. He was certainly getting a phone call tomorrow.

Right now, he needed to hunt down the man responsible.

Jake turned to the British agent and scowled.

"What targets do we have to consider?" he asked. "Right this second, Nathaniel is moving in to hit whoever it was he has selected, so we don't have much time to intercept him."

He followed the man to the center tripod. A one hundred-mile radius, with all manner of rings marked, plus an entire legend of locations, none of which were identified. George and Hollyanne flanked them.

Why he thought fifty miles, Jake could not say. Except that an inner ring of twenty miles generally included Birmingham and all its satellite towns and suburbs and could be gotten to easily, even with traffic. Leicester was about forty miles, with Worcester about thirty. Northampton was fifty, give or take.

"Lots," Steve said. "We've been bashing our skulls against a wall trying to figure out what he might hit, me and George. The Undersecretary was assuming a Mass Casualty Incident, but as you might have surmised, some of the more experienced agents have a low opinion of that sort of thing."

"You're approaching it all wrong," Jake said, smiling to take the sting out of his words. "Assuming it's Nathaniel, and we are, he wants something valuable, electronic, and portable. Spencer, you pretend to be Nathaniel for now."

Jake nearly laughed out loud when Spencer looked up from his keyboard and a hard, bitter scowl came across the man's face. His shoulders hunched a little forward and his eyes got all squinty.

"I'll teach that bastard McNeil," he snarled in a dead-perfect imitation of the voice they all remembered.

Spencer rose from his chair and started to pace, hands clenched behind him. Jake grabbed the two English agents and quickly dragged them out of the way and back from the three maps.

"I've been in prison for a while," Spencer announced in a hard, angry voice. "Missed being able to manipulate bitcoin and the other block-chain currencies, or I'd have had enough money to buy Kent and have everyone evicted. English Kent, not Seattle Kent, mind you."

That got a laugh. Kent near Seattle was a manufacturing suburb on the way to Tacoma, eating all the fields that had once fed both cities as folks moved south and warehouses sprang up. English Kent was a good chunk of the southeast of the country.

"I need **money**," Spencer continued with a dead-perfect growl. "Need a big hit that will convince people

I'm still a player, as well as set me up for future games. I need to announce to the world that I'M BACK!!!"

"Hit a bank?" George asked before anyone said anything.

"Pocket change!" Spencer roared. "Unless you have a gold bullion warehouse, not even worth stealing a truck to drive there. You got any of those around?"

He'd ended up right in front of the new agent, scowling up at the man from close in.

"Gold?" Jake asked Steve.

"London or certain military bases," Steve replied. "Rather like Fort Knox, in the States. Plus, one facility up near Edinburgh that we don't talk about, but too far away to consider now."

Spencer nodded.

"This is not a caper movie with fast cars and witty banter, gentlemen," he announced in a grand voice. "I want to get away afterwards. I want something far more portable. Information, mind you. Something good that I can copy and sell many times. Maybe hold for ransom from the government as well and get them to pay for it at the same time I sell it to some friends on the dark web. Plus the Russians are always willing to send me gold for English secrets. What have you got, boys?"

Jake watched the two British agents turn to each other in confusion.

"Information?" George asked.

"Something like a super-secret data center," Hollyanne spoke up. "Where the Ministry perhaps dumps backups to tape across a big pipeline, like the big Tech Firms in Seattle do to places like Chelan and that."

Jake doubted that even something like *East of the Mountains* would mean anything to these two men, but then, all of England was physically about thirty percent smaller than just Washington State, albeit with eight times the population.

Steve stopped and considered things for a long moment, one hand over his mouth and rubbing his chin. He had a bit of stubble going, but Jake guessed that the man had been possibly running for two days solid now. Maybe three, with catnaps.

Jake followed Steve to the ring map and watched him consider something. Finally, he seemed to find something on the map and Jake watched his face turn confused.

"Data Center," Steve said. "What would he expect to find at a data center?"

"Personnel files let you know who might be blackmailable," Jake said. "Operations files might contain information and plans that could be sold to other people. Even land planning can be profitable. If you know where the government wants to build, you can buy the land cheap now and wait."

"Wouldn't that stuff be encrypted?" George asked.

Spencer's evil laugh interrupted Jake's comment.

"You think they'll actually take the time to hash that data at the London end before transmission?" Spencer snarled in Nathaniel's voice. "Oh, please. Probably store entire databases in clear text uncompressed because it takes too long to compress, and some Important Bureaucrat wants it done NOW!"

"Hey, you…" George started to say, but Steve waved a hand in his face.

"You can go sit in the damned car, if you think that will protect you tomorrow," Steve snarled angrily at his partner.

Everyone flinched at the man's tone. Jake assumed too much coffee and stress, mixed with no sleep. And maybe his career hanging in front of him if Sir William had personally reached out to the man.

"What have you got?" Jake asked.

Steve's whole face seemed to squint for a moment.

"The Ministry opened a new spot in the middle of nowhere, about a year ago," the man said. "And I mean nowhere, but we've got people supposed to keep watch. Secure facility, the kind with hardened doors around an office building, and not armed patrols with dogs outside or anything. Low profile. Just racks and racks of computers and what some wag called barrels to hold data, instead of buckets. Getting anywhere close to the place would set off all sorts of alarms."

"Where?" Jake asked.

"Southeast of Banbury," Steve replied nervously. "Place called King's Sutton. Little bit east of the north end of the Cotswolds. Pain in the ass to get in and out of, although the M40 runs close. You still have to run up this tiny lane to get to the town itself, and the roads are your typical English village twisty."

"Show me," Rik was suddenly standing next to them, looming over the two agents.

Didn't feel like that tonight, though. Steve blinked at her in surprise and his hand found a spot on the map.

"What have you got?" Jake asked the woman.

"Been studying local transportation networks," Rik smiled. "Oxford Canal runs right by there. Easy enough to slip a narrow boat right close in the dead of night and offload a crew of troublemakers."

Jake turned to Steve.

"I'm guessing your standard playbook calls for road-blocks to go up everywhere and random inspections of motor traffic, doesn't it?" he asked as the man's face paled and he nodded. "And we wouldn't be able to get there in any sort of hurry, would we?"

"Impossible," Steve whispered.

"Are there any other spots we think fall into this category?" Spencer asked, back to himself as another data nerd.

"Nothing at all," Steve said. "The other interesting targets are all in Birmingham proper."

"Jake?" Hollyanne asked.

"We've got one shot at this," he informed the others. "Grant, you roll with Steve and George and get there when you can, but you're the communications nexus."

"Got it," Grant nodded.

"You're up, Rik," Jake turned to her and smiled. "Let's get crazy."

CHAPTER

TWENTY-NINE

NATHANIEL FOUND something utterly quintessential about riding in an English narrow boat. Sure, other countries did similar things, but in many places around here the water was barely three feet deep in such a canal. You could walk across with dry hair if you were careful. And yet they went everywhere.

Everywhere.

He had more than once considered acquiring a boat like this one, just to have a lovely little vacation spot that moved around, but that would have to wait until such a time as he had a new identity that the English weren't pursuing.

He was seated inside of the semi-dark aft cabin, letting Tommy and the rest deal with things while he held himself aloof and imperious. One mission tonight and he could go back to hiding forever in the shadows while he sent out others, but he really didn't have the staff he needed for a major operation.

Monday: Recruiting. No, strike that. Wednesday. Monday, he'd still be in hiding and running if all went well.

The door opened and Lucky stuck his dark head through the gap with a bright smile.

"Time, sir," he said quietly.

Nathaniel nodded and grabbed the black messenger bag that went with his dark clothes, hefting it and slinging it across his back, with a new laptop and other equipment that he would need for tonight's adventure.

He turned and followed the man forward with a fierce smile on his face. Tommy was already on the bow, and they were close enough to hop directly to the shore, so he moved as soon as Nathaniel emerged, matching Nathaniel's smile with his own. Then it was onto dry land, and across a small bridge that covered the original stream to which this canal had been added later.

Darkness surrounded them, along with night sounds. The highway was close, but only a few cars were rushing back to London tonight for Monday morning, and the last train had already run.

He followed the other two and began to walk.

NATHANIEL SMILED in the darkness as they crept along the edge of some farmer's field. The target looked like just another farmhouse, which is what it had been before the government had secretly bought the place and dug an underground vault in the guise of general renovations.

Everyone thought a Pakistani billionaire had quietly acquired the entire farm as a bolt-hole to escape his homeland, and there was even an agent of the right ethnicity and background who came round regularly like an absentee landlord. Quiet, rural England would ignore the man as an outsider, which was really anyone whose great-grandparents weren't born in the village.

Tommy had the lead, squishing quietly along in dark clothes with a bag over his shoulder that contained the armaments the man felt he might need. Lucky was trailing behind, because a tall, skinny black man would absolutely stand out around here. Nathaniel was in the middle, dressed like something of a country squire who had been out shooting today and not changed afterwards. And he could sound like a toff if anyone challenged them before they arrived.

The other half-dozen men of the team were back on the boat, moored for the night and all set to slip away quietly with night vision goggles that would let them navigate the canal while the police were busy checking cars.

Mill Lane emerged from the trees in front of them, and Nathaniel could see the old cemetery on his right not far away through more trees and around the curve in the road.

Just another farmhouse on the edge of King's Sutton. Quaint. Remote. Quiet.

You had to know what had been done here to appreciate the amount of money involved.

Nathaniel counted cars in the driveway. His sources had said two staff were on duty all weekend, with a different crew arriving in the morning and working Monday to Friday morning and then switching off again.

Technicians, not even bureaucrats. Former military intelligence, certainly, but not special forces commandos by any stretch. Nerds like him.

"All good, gov'nor," Tommy murmured quietly as they watched.

Nathaniel had to agree. Now, the hard part.

They crossed the road to where the hedge on this side

thinned some. There was an old stream bed that Tommy had been following, though the water itself had long since been rerouted around the property, and a sludge pit that was probably kept around for verisimilitude.

Into the 'backyard' where they quickly worked their way through some bushes to where a driveway wrapped all the way around the back. The place still looked like a farm run by tenants, but Nathaniel wasn't the least bit fooled.

"You sure about this?" Tommy asked, just a bit hesitantly.

"I paid good bribes for this information," Nathaniel replied a bit tartly. "They'd have already arrested us if they knew we were coming. Plus, everyone will be turned to look at Birmingham right about now."

"Right," Lucky broke in cheerily. "Let's go."

The tall man had a natural camouflage at night, so Nathaniel followed. He was also far more technically inclined than a hooligan like Tommy. The back door to the old cellar was right where it was supposed to be and had the exact ten-key security badge reader Nathaniel had expected, carefully obscured.

Nathaniel pulled out a small bottle of spray paint and hit the two cameras that had a view of this nook. Without lights on, nobody should have seen them get this close. Now, they couldn't.

Lucky knelt next to the card reader and pulled out a couple of tools.

Quickly enough, he had the face off the reader and studied the innards. Nathaniel understood motherboards in the abstract, but hadn't gone into electrical engineering, as all the colleges had finally moved those majors into computer science by then and focused on teaching programming languages instead.

Plus, he had experts in locks he could call on.

Lucky had the door quietly unlocked in about ten seconds. He looked up and smiled.

"We're in," he said. "As soon as you open that door, a local alarm will go off, but hopefully nothing off-site."

"Right, then," Tommy smiled, pulling a black Glock pistol from his bag. "Let's drop by for a spot of tea, shall we?"

Nathaniel nodded as well and let the two men lead. His job was to stay out of the way while the locals were apprehended. Only then could he start his work.

One quick glance and right about now the night sky of Birmingham should have been split by a bomb, followed by everyone who could rushing in and getting in everyone's way. Even the M40 just across the way would be marked with at least cursory roadblocks, even this far out.

But Nathaniel wasn't leaving that way. Nothing that would leave a trace.

Tommy put a hand on the door, glanced back, then pulled it open, leading with his pistol.

Mudroom, of sorts, when Nathaniel followed. Coats on hooks and Wellies off to one side.

A red light flashed silently over the next door, but Nathaniel already knew that time was now running through the hourglass quickly. In and out and gone.

Tommy turned left and entered a transverse hallway. Well lit. Offices on the right. Closed doors leading to bedrooms, bathrooms, and a kitchen.

Nathaniel could hear voices ahead. Tommy and Lucky moved in near silence.

"What do they think happened?" a higher-pitched voice asked. Male. Thirties from the tone.

"Bomb of some sort in Birmingham," a lower voice replied. Also male. Older and heavier, perhaps. "Teams are scrambling everywhere, and an alert has gone out."

"Hey, that's a local alarm!" the first voice piped up.

"Right you are, governor," Tommy said, standing suddenly in the door with the Glock out and pointed. "Don't do anything rash and you'll live to see daylight, right?"

Lucky was close but watching the hall around them. Like Tommy, he'd brought a pistol, but this was all for show. Hopefully, those men didn't feel the need to die for Queen and Country tonight.

"Stand up slowly and hands in the air," Tommy growled.

Nathaniel slipped close and found two men in black uniforms that he would have called rent-a-cops in Seattle. Military haircuts, but neither could pass a physical fitness test right now, let alone run a combat obstacle course in anything less than days. Pudgy and bordering on fat, respectively.

"This is a robbery, not an assassination," Nathaniel assured them. "Face the wall so you can be handcuffed, and we'll be gone fairly quickly, okay?"

Both men complied. Neither had a holster on their belt. According to Nathaniel's spies and bribes, the guns were here, but locked in a box under the long desk where two men sat watching monitors and status checks on various things.

One of them had been watching porn on either an unsecured channel or from a local datastore. Probably the latter, as Nathaniel couldn't imagine that level of gap in firewall security in a place like this. Better to just upload an entire library of videos and books to entertain the men. As far as Nathaniel had been able to determine, the staff was all male, so that sort of thing might be allowed when someone was trapped in here for days without seeing the sun.

Lucky entered the small office now as the two men

faced the wall and got them both cuffed. Then he and Tommy moved them to the break room to be out of Nathaniel's way. Fortunately, they hadn't even had a chance to lock their workstations, not that it would have taken Nathaniel more than five minutes to crack something like that.

Having direct access just meant that he could see progress indicators. He already had the usernames and passwords he needed to gain administrative access to this system.

Bored, lonely, and underpaid was no way to treat your staff, but this Ministry had fallen for the American way of outsourcing things to a civilian company that skimmed the money and paid their staff far less than they were worth.

Much easier to offer someone ten thousand pounds for the information you needed when they might only make forty thousand this year. And it let the man Nathaniel had turned feel better about screwing the people who'd been screwing him, because they would lose the contract tomorrow, but the staff would just be hired by someone else with little operational change.

An endless carousel of corruption and malfeasance that nobody at the top seemed intelligent enough to break. Or willing to.

Nathaniel's life would get much harder if there were honest actors, but that was never happening, so he reviewed the current status of things. Rather than pull the full laptop from his bag, he just grabbed the portable hard drive out of the side pocket and plugged it in.

Again, in a truly secured facility, those might have been glued shut and then the wires cut, but these men needed to be able to air-gap things, so most of what got onto local systems had to be handloaded. Of course, without permissions, you'd be fired for what Nathaniel was in the act of doing, but those men could honestly say that they'd been captured before they knew what was happening and then immediately removed from the room.

Hell, he might be able to use one of them next time he needed to gain access to a secure facility somewhere, just from the way they were going to be treated by government agents tomorrow.

Fools.

A pop-up form appeared on the screen.

Warning: Unauthorized data connection detected.

The bottom of the box had a place for him to type the administrative user and this month's password, after which the box vanished, and a new window showed him a new *T:/* drive in with all the existing network drives representing other facilities and systems remote to this one.

With more time, Nathaniel might have used this console to try to access some of those, but that would take more hours than he had until someone needed to check in with some authority.

No, better to hit and run. Get what he needed and disappear, so that he could turn it into money that would fund the sort of rebuilding of his wider operation that Nathaniel Hoestler needed to break back into the big time. Make his mark on the world.

Rub Jake and Pacific Force's faces in the fact that he'd finally beaten them and gotten away.

Nathaniel browsed until he found the backup he wanted. There was a tape drive in the corner with a stack of blanks on a shelf above it, but that was yesterday's sequential backup on top of last week's full. Better to grab the new weekly backup that had just spent an hour being transmitted from London.

There. Nathaniel typed a few commands, maneuvered to the files he wanted, and started a copy to the HDD resting on the desk. He leaned back as the system told him zero percent complete and started a little ball spinning.

It would take an hour, but he had everyone looking the wrong way right now.

Misdirection. And then escape.

Victory, for once.

RIK WAS SO excited that she wondered if she might actually glow in the dark if someone were to turn the lights off here in the aft cabin. Twin propellers cut the night with a roaring hum on a cantilevered wing overhead, but the plane was up high enough that the night sky was silent otherwise.

Clouds overhead blocked out some of the stars, but not enough to matter. Moon low on the horizon lighting things. Not enough to read by, but enough to hunt by if you were careful.

And hungry.

Everyone was suited up for the jump. Helmets and goggles. Parachutes packed by someone she trusted.

The jumpmaster opened the door and the noise trebled.

"Everyone stand by," the jumpmaster called loudly.

Jake was close by Rik. Spencer and Hollyanne rose from where they had been sitting and stepped into line.

"This is where I remind you that what you are doing is the second most insane thing I can think of," the man yelled over the noise of the props.

"What's first, Nigel?" Rik yelled back.

"Not until the statute of limitations expires, young lady," he laughed.

"Coward," she laughed with him.

She'd known Nigel for more than a decade, having first learned how to skydive from the man before taking that knowledge and *requiring* the rest of the team know how to do it. Nobody else did it as a hobby, but they were much more boring than she was anyway.

Over the open door, a red light turned yellow, and Nigel moved to stand immediately next to the door itself. He looked out the gap just enough to confirm something in his own head before turning to her.

"Last chance to abort," Nigel yelled at her.

"Last chance to jump with us," she yelled back. "We're committed."

"Negative on that," he said. "Someone has to survive this and tell the authorities where to look when you break a leg landing."

"All fields around here," Jake yelled.

"Plowed fields." Nigel turned to him. "And the river and the canal. Plus, whatever else you hit. Remember that the ground might be so soft you stick the landing and break an ankle, so roll anyway and abandon the gear. I am already going to come back for it tomorrow, plus you paid for the damage insurance."

Rik smiled and laughed just for the hell of it.

The yellow light began to blink green now.

"FIVE SECONDS!" Nigel roared.

Rik took a deep breath, released it, and then drew another one in.

She was already moving at a dead run when the light stopped blinking, a monotonous, green orb announcing the village of King's Sutton passing below them right now.

"AND JUMP!" She heard Nigel call, but Rik was already free-falling by the time he got the words out.

Again, second most insane for Nigel maybe made her top ten this year, but she wasn't about to tell him that. The other three would be diving into the night sky with her as fast as they could move.

The ground wasn't that far away, and she had already programmed everyone's altimeter to pull the ripcord not that far above the minimum safe jump.

If Nathaniel was down there, Pacific Force needed to land on his head.

Narrow boats were nice and everything if you wanted quiet.

Rik was in a hurry.

JAKE WATCHED the tall blond leap into eternity and tried to catch her. He missed but knew that he'd be relatively close to her when they got down. Each helmet had a small marker light blinking on the back, and he picked her up, below and ahead.

There was no time for showing off, so he pulled arms and legs tight against his body and arrowed down. Hollyanne would do the same. Spencer might lag, but he wasn't expected to rush immediately into combat on the ground anyway. Not like the other three.

Spencer was the spotter. The photojournalist who sat off to one side and gathered evidence. Rik had her bow broken down and stored in a small satchel along with half a dozen arrows. He and Hollyanne could go toe to toe with anyone, assuming nobody brought machine guns.

The night was silent compared to the roar of the aircraft, already rapidly receding. Cooler, too, but that would change as they got to the ground.

Jake picked up the long black stripe of the combined river and canal and railroad, running west of the village. The M40 highway was even further west, but they had been crossing NW to SE, so their target zone would put them hopefully in a field just a quarter mile south of the farmhouse, not that far from the cemetery he'd seen marked on the maps before they took off.

Grant would be racing here with the others, but they wouldn't make great progress, having to cross all of the Birmingham metroplex in this mess, coming down from Manchester where Pacific Force had left the jet.

If it hadn't been the middle of the night, so to speak, there were other runways that could have been used to land, but none close enough, save for a weird, triangular field used for skydiving and other sports rather than anything commercial. No lights and no controller, plus it was about three miles away from the target, and they'd be coming in without a vehicle to get them that last distance.

As Rik had said, completely insane, but fast. That was going to be the critical part.

The chute opened right on time, slowing him with heavy jar. Jake's hands went up and automatically found the handles he needed to steer.

They were about to fall out of the sky as fast as they could, guided by the moonlight and the nearby village's glow, and rendezvous at the cemetery just long enough to make their stalk. He was being carried a little east and south by the breeze, but that was just another large field.

Below, a single vehicle illuminated Mill Lane as it drove south from the village. Jake had a momentary spike of terror that it might turn in at the farmhouse, but it kept going.

There was just enough glow from everything that Jake could see the trees starting to get serious about leaves, but not the heavier cover they would provide come summer. He saw a ghost nearby and realized that Hollyanne had caught up with him, and they would land almost simultaneously, like a competitive performance sport of synchronized skydiving.

He drew in a breath as he got close, mindful of what Nigel had said about plowed fields being too soft on landing for you to expect to hit running. Jake blew everything out and allowed himself to crumble up in a ball and roll a little as the ground reached out and caught him.

Soft. Freshly plowed and sown, if he had to guess. Hopefully the seeds were just getting going and he hadn't left a Jake-sized hole in what would grow later. He caught his breath and grabbed lines, pulling everything into a ball. The breeze he'd had above had fallen to almost nothing here, so the chute was relatively easy to gather up.

Jake got everything into a bundle, wrapped the cords around it quickly, and stripped the helmet, goggles, and jumpsuit off, adding them to the pile.

He had a rendezvous with someone and didn't feel like making Nathaniel wait.

THIRTY-TWO

HOLLYANNE MOVED up to the hedge surrounding the cemetery a little ahead of Jake, but she'd been in a hurry. Rik was already there on the southeast corner, so she moved towards the woman, the two of them watching the farmhouse across the two fields and various hedges.

Spencer actually arrived at the same time as Jake. She turned to them both.

"Anything?" Jake asked.

"Quiet," Rik offered. "No idea if alarms would be external, but I doubt it. If you needed help here, it needed to come from someplace larger and specialized, so Birmingham would be my guess. No police constable would be of much use in this sort of problem."

Hollyanne noted that the woman had assembled her bow already but was carrying it with one of those blunt, stun-tips nocked. Taking prisoners. Useful to know, unless she'd only had the one flash/bang and had used it last night.

You had to be careful what you smuggled into England. Even Pacific Force could only bend the rules so far.

Jake paused a little longer before he spoke, but from his body language, he wasn't going to put her in charge of this phase. They'd discussed it while getting ready but made no decisions.

"Rik, you lead the stalk," Jake announced in a quiet voice. "Spencer, you have the rear wing flank. Hollyanne and I will have wingback positions inside. Remember that we've presumably got help coming down from Northampton, once those folks get rerouted from their original plan to flood the place, but no cops will be vectored down onto this location until we call them in or someone inside triggers a panic button."

"Everyone set phones on silent-only mode," Rik said. "We'll move fast but we are functionally out of radio contact from this moment, so don't even bring them out to check time or messages until I say, because I need the darkness, and we don't know where the cameras are. I am shooting on movement and expecting Hollyanne and Jake to take down anyone I engage immediately afterwards. Spencer, you can record audio for later. Questions?"

"None," Hollyanne replied glancing at the others.

"Let's move."

And Rik was off.

They moved along the rear hedge of the cemetery and then pushed their way through another hedge into the field just north of it. This field was also plowed and planted, but looking back, there was no light to reveal them, so Hollyanne wasn't surprised when Rik cut straight across, angling in on the target.

Maps had been a bit iffy and out of date, so they had to rely on experience and guts from here. Rik got them to a spot where a stream ran, winding a little as it moved, but not that deep a cut into the land. There was a greater chance of turning an ankle than anything, but they all crossed easily enough and ended up crouched down in a weird backyard.

Or maybe it was normal. Hollyanne hadn't grown up on a farm, so she had no idea what farmers kept behind the house. That might be a garden that wasn't awake yet. Or maybe had been a garden and nobody kept it up these days since it was impossible to see unless you were already trespassing like this.

"Front or rear?" Rik asked now, glancing at the others as they watched.

To Hollyanne, it looked perfectly normal, but Steve had assured them that the Ministry had actually spent a lot of money specifically to maintain that illusion.

"Is that a driveway?" Hollyanne asked Jake.

Spencer pointed a 35mm camera that she presumed had a night lens on it.

"It is," he replied after a moment. "There is a door that looks like a storm cellar, down a couple of steps on the right. Closed but that doesn't mean anything."

"Rik, can you get a good shooting stand to cover the door?" Jake asked.

Hollyanne studied the terrain but knew that she would probably be going first through the door if they penetrated the facility.

"Maybe, but it will be crowded," Rik replied.

"Spencer's coming in, so it will be just you," Jake assured her.

"Oh, then yeah," Rik said. "On the right there, where you see that 55-gallon drum. At night, I'd look like a second one butted up against it until I moved."

"Okay, you move there when we move forward," Jake said. "You text Steve updates and cover our back in case we somehow got here ahead of Nathaniel. And handle any runners, like London."

"On it."

Rik seemed to vibrate with an energy almost as great as Hollyanne's, but Hollyanne was always like this in those last ten seconds before she descended into flow state and began katas and combat.

"Hollyanne, you lead," Jake said. "Spencer in the middle."

She nodded now and rose like a fog flowing across a Scottish moor, letting that dark spot draw her like a moth seeking the opposite of flame. Hollyanne heard the others behind her, but she was absolutely one with the night.

Across the driveway and up a small sidewalk, she paused, kneeling down to look for sensors or wires hidden in the grass on either side. She didn't expect the British government to do anything like that, nor Nathaniel, but she wouldn't really know that they'd guessed right until some-thing went very wrong.

Or right.

Seeing nothing, she rose again and moved forward like fog rolling in. Down two steps and into a dark spot.

Hollyanne raised a hand to pause the others.

The smell told her everything she needed, even before she saw the locking mechanism torn open and hanging by a wire.

"We're right," she said simply in a low voice. "Someone spray painted the cameras recently enough that the paint hasn't dried. Plus, the locks are broken. Spencer, you're on."

THIRTY-THREE

SPENCER DIDN'T DIVE into combat with the others very often. By training and inclination, he was best suited to be Rik's spotter, finding targets and watching her back.

But he was also the most experienced with electronic security systems. He knelt now and pulled a Leatherman from a pocket, flipping open the flathead screwdriver tip as a useful universal tool to do things. A pocket flash no bigger than his pinkie finger got turned on and handed up to Jake to hold while he worked.

Someone had popped the casing open with a similar tool, as it was just resting in place on tabs. Inside, they had done the same thing he was doing right now, tracing leads and looking for the signal to tell the door to open.

Stupid board, designed to be generic and installed in ten million locations. Spencer would have at least secured the outer casing with some sort of screw tip with a compli- cated pattern that nobody carried as part of a standard kit. The kind that you made people strip and chew up and maybe make a lot of noise to access.

But he was all about denying access to places.

Whoever had budgeted for this facility had either been naturally cheap or had gotten a kickback from the installers, because they'd gone cheap in the one place you shouldn't.

"I can open it," he said over his shoulder. "They still in there?"

"Either they are and we're in combat immediately, or they're gone and we rescue hostages left behind," Jake said now. "You get set to unlock the door, Spencer. I'll open it. Hollyanne will go through first, then me. You come through but stay three steps back and mostly just keep us from being surprised from the rear."

"Gotcha," Spencer said, rising, and getting organized.

Touch the flathead here and you'll bridge the circuit to open the locks. Probably set off an alarm, but how close would anyone be paying attention?

Jake handed him the light and moved to the door, putting one hand on the handle.

Hollyanne had gone into that place where she was a Valkyrie about to pounce on you from the night sky, but she did that.

"Counting down," Spencer said in a low voice. "Four. Three. Two. One. Contact."

He touched the spot and the locks thunked open. Jake grabbed the door and pulled.

Hollyanne *moved*.

HOLLYANNE WENT through the open door with more noise than she wanted but understanding that the trade-off was for speed. Nathaniel would be paying attention to his perimeter if an alarm went off right now.

Anyone other than Nathaniel in charge and they'd probably have someone more or less standing just inside the door beyond to slow her down. Not that it would slow her for long, but the noise of taking someone apart might alert the others.

She'd one-punch going by and let Jake finish them. They made a good team that way.

But the vestibule was empty. Muddy boots and jackets that were hung from pegs. Hallway beyond.

The door had been on the right end of the building, looking at it from the back, so she automatically turned left and looked around the corner. Nobody in immediate sight but two doors open of the five she could see, with lights from both.

Hollyanne flipped a coin in her head and went for the door on the left as she faced them. Jake would take the right. Spencer would stay mostly back at this transverse hallway and run interference against anyone coming from the lone door on the right.

This was not their first rodeo, as Rik would have said were she down here with them.

Fast as Hollyanne was, she saw a shadow appear at the threshold to the door as she moved. Someone inside the room had stood up or moved from right to left, with an overhead light casting a shadow into the hallway.

She risked a fast glance to the right and saw what she presumed was the office that was the target of this entire operation, with another shape seated and working.

"Hey, we just got an intruder—" the man approaching the door was saying.

As soon as he spoke, she had exploded forward.

A gun appeared at the doorway, waist high as if being carried in a ready position. Glock. Large frame version. Average height male. Growling, East End accent. Baritone.

Tommy?

They reached the doorway at the same moment. Hollyanne reached out with her right hand and batted the pistol up and away with the back of her wrist using a crane form. Greater reach and she didn't need a lot of power.

Just deflection, which was good because the man triggered a shot into the ceiling as he flinched.

Hollyanne completed the move and drove an elbow upwards and across into his side, bruising ribs and jarring the man hard as she did.

Indeed Tommy. The bulldog who was one of Nathaniel's top thugs. Air was exploding out of his lungs already as she grabbed his right wrist with her left hand and continued the motion to lift the weapon.

His weight made a good anchor, so she caught one of his ankles with her foot and let that give her a pivot point. Hollyanne wasn't playing nice and didn't know how many more men and guns Nathaniel might have brought with her.

Tommy triggered a second shot into the ceiling as she punched him in the balls as hard as she could. The sound escaping the man's mouth was pure horror, a bandsaw being ground against a steel bar and losing teeth as sparks went everywhere.

Movement beyond caused her to drop to a crouch with Tommy as he fell. Three men in the room beyond. Two appeared handcuffed or something on a couch while an incredibly tall black man rose from a chair and lifted a pistol to shoot her.

JAKE MEMORIZED the interior of the basement as he trailed in Hollyanne's wake. She went left so he automatically crossed to the right. Two doors that would need to be secured simultaneously, with Spencer just this side of the entry hallway from the sound of his shoes on the tile floor underfoot.

Hollyanne made no sound. Jake didn't make much.

He saw the gunman at the same time that Hollyanne did, but Jake had to stay on his side of the corridor for now. Plus, they still had surprise, at least for another moment or two.

Gunshot as Jake got close to the doorway, but he'd already seen her moving to take the man on. Second blow, followed by a third. From the scream, you might think that the man was being gelded. And it probably felt something like that when she did it, but anyone carrying a gun in England had already gotten up this morning and decided that he wanted to be regarded as a dangerous lunatic killer.

America had too many guns, but the laws allowed it and were extremely permissive about carrying in most places, especially the farther west you got.

Jake rounded the corner a heartbeat after the first gunshot and just had time to register Nathaniel seated and rising when the second shot went off amidst the other pad. No crushing blow to his back, so she'd taken her man down, and he needed to do the same here.

Nathaniel's face was a hard growl of pure rage cast in flesh.

They had often been mistaken for brothers when they were younger. More than one person had compared Jake's bones to a Nagel print, with those angular lines.

Nathaniel Hoestler had a longer, more rectangular face with a squarer jaw. His cheekbones were more shallow and rounded, but close enough that to Jake it was like staring in a funhouse mirror.

Only the difference in haircuts really marked them different.

Jake had enough time to take in two monitors, both unlocked but the closer one not doing anything. Long, flat desk with coffee mugs and empty Coke cans on the nearer one. Corporate office chairs. Soft, moss-colored walls designed to sooth on a long stint in front of a boring system.

Then Nathaniel was on him. If the faces were similar, the bodies were the same. Nathaniel was his height and weight within tiny variations. Same reach.

There was no space to maneuver in here, but Jake had the advantage because he just had to delay things. There was backup behind him in Hollyanne and Spencer. Rik was outside with her bow. Grant was riding south with the cavalry.

If they could just get here in time.

Nathaniel took one beat too long by shoving the chair between them under the desk, giving Jake that blink to drop into stance, hands up defending. He was letting

Nathaniel have the edge, but the man didn't have a pistol, so it would be fists.

As with everything then, even.

But Jake was willing to stack his team up against Nathaniel's every day of the week, because he had Pacific Force, and Hoestler just had a bunch of hooligans and mercenaries.

Nathaniel growled as he threw a punch. Mostly a feint, but there was enough force behind it if it connected. Everything was a threat on so many levels that Jake let his brain disengage and everything became, as his instructor had said it in heavily-Vietnamese-accented English "Au-to-mat-**TIQUE**!"

Jake blocked and flowed inward, shifting enough that his counterpunch was also blocked, but neither man betrayed his balance.

A knee came up and Jake slid past it enough that it would maybe raise a welt, but not even a bruise.

He pivoted an elbow in and forced Nathaniel to lift a shoulder to blunt it.

Tighter. Closer.

Both men planted their feet and let arms and hips work. Anyone lifting a foot at this point, even for the blink of an eye, would sacrifice balance. Either they would be lifted backwards or jerked down. In these confined spaces, either would be fatal. Well, not fatal, but eminently stupid.

Jake listened with half an ear to the noise behind him, but couldn't determine what was happening, and then it was just grapple and strike, over and over, twisting in and out like two weasels covered in grease.

Jake just had to buy time.

HOLLYANNE DIDN'T THINK about what she was doing. Thought would only slow her down at this point.

She still held Tommy's Glock by the barrel as Lucky began processing what he was seeing. Didn't look like he had trained on this sort of thing, because he was moving wrong, standing to shoot at her instead of attacking.

Hollyanne snapped the pistol at Lucky's head like she would a Frisbee, trusting that his flinch would be sufficient. At the other end of the throw, it had to look like someone had just tossed a black cat at you.

She actually trained occasionally with someone trying to hit her with racquetballs in an enclosed space, just to get used to that sort of silliness, but Hollyanne's approach to every single day was that time not spent training was probably time wasted.

She came off the floor behind the flying pistol. Lucky had indeed flinched.

She heard the distinct click of the trigger being pulled, but the man hadn't flipped the safety off first. Would have missed her anyway, because he had lifted his hands to protect himself from the thing his eyes had interpreted as that cat coming right at him.

At least he had some level of brains. Rather than try to shoot her, he swung his own pistol like a hammer at her. Hollyanne put her shortness to advantage now and went low after a knee.

The dude had arms and legs like a crane, going on forever. Hollyanne didn't use crane forms all that often, because her compactness worked better when she got in close with someone.

She struck the closest knee with the back of a fist, whipping it hard as she moved under the blow and a little past the man. That hammer came down but missed as he cracked his forearm on her shoulder blade. Probably hurt him more than her, because she knew it was coming and he was entirely out of position.

Hollyanne used her momentum to cross under and behind the punk now. Someone had given him an understanding of the martial arts because he stepped away from her as he tried to turn. Probably still thinking that he could shoot her in the confusion.

She placed everything in the room now as she reversed field. Couch with two hostages behind her on the left. Round table for dining closer to this side of the room but not all that crowded. Lucky had been sitting on the far side from the prisoners. Tommy had likely been standing, as the other chairs were pushed in.

Kitchenette sort of thing taking up the entire right side as she began to move, with a fridge, a stove, and a microwave, plus a small sink and a dishwasher. All the comforts of home when you're trapped here for days on end.

Hollyanne smiled at Lucky Sokoro. Tall. Skinny. He really did look like the dangerous Masai warriors of Kenya in overall shape, but tonight he was dressed like a punk off the London docks in black pants, T-shirt, and an overshirt not heavy enough to be considered a jacket.

Then she was on him.

Fool was still concentrating on shooting her. She heard him find the safety and struck for the arm and hand holding it. Turned this way, he was likely to hit the two men behind her if he fired a shot, so she ignored his other hand coming to grab her and punched him right where those long fingers were wrapped around the pistol.

The sound of impact was maybe similar to closing your fingers in a car door accidentally.

Had it been an accident.

Hell of a stinger.

Hollyanne absorbed a punch in the top of her head as the cost of controlling the gun. Tall guy lost control of the weapon and that was all she needed. Gravity took over from there, and she went after his knee again.

Not in a position to break his shin, she just lit him up with a stinger again as she blinked a few times. She didn't remember him having any serious muscles, but he apparently did. Or he'd gotten lucky.

Hollyanne dropped and rolled away from him in a fast somersault to pop up next to the couch.

Tall, lucky guy had tried to step into a punch but discovered that his lower leg might have just gone a little numb.

Whoops.

She smiled up at all of his six foot four inches, give or take. Two heads taller than her. Almost as angry. Built like a black stork that had gone slightly lame.

He hobbled in her direction and threw a jab. Probably used to having incredible reach when he did that. Hollyanne let it come, watching with enormous eyes, and then falling perhaps an inch to her left and just touching the back of his wrist to deflect the blow past her ear with nothing more than a whoosh of air.

Long, gangly arms meant he did have an extra bit of advantage keeping her at bay, so she slid in behind the fist and gripped the bone with her blocking hand, anchoring it just enough that she could slide her right arm up in a snake form. She looped around his arm once and then sank her weight into the floor, using those extra fifteen inches to pull him forward off-balance.

Water buffalo normally was the perfect follow-up once you had someone anchored like this, but he was too far away for her to connect with that elbow, so she had to punch him instead.

This was where it got tricky. The forehead was the hardest bone in the human body, designed to be bashed. The top of the skull was pretty good as well. Coming at the sides, it was fairly easy to kill someone by rupturing all the fragile bones around the eyes and pushing then into the brain cavity.

He might have it coming from drawing a pistol on her and shooting randomly, but Nathaniel had also taken the two men in this facility prisoner and had his goons watching them, when another villain could have just as easily killed them at the top in order to keep them out of his way.

All that in a flash as she transitioned her flow state from Death to merely Avenger, one arm anchoring this lucky son of a bitch in place.

She opened her palm and slapped the man as hard as she could rotate her hips right now. The sound was comparable to a gunshot in the close confines of the room.

His eyes got big with shock and surprise and his entire body went slack for a moment, so she reversed her pivot and drove her right knee into his stomach. Not as good as a punch, but she'd caught him off guard again and all the air rushed out of his lungs.

Then he fell forward and she released her snake grip. The other painful spot on the skull is right behind and below the ears on both sides, where all the nerves cluster. She poked him with three fingers right there as he went by and she watched him lay flat out, a black stork in death like some piece of Renaissance art.

He wasn't dead, but she'd gotten the blow perfect for once, and he was as far out as if she'd sapped him. Close enough to identical.

No time to deal with anything, she grabbed both pistols off the floor like throwing knives and set the safeties. She turned to the door and glanced out before emerging.

Spencer was close, watching like he was supposed to, covering her rear flank.

"Here," she said, stepping close and pressing a Glock into his hand.

They hadn't brought anything but Rik's bow, and Spencer wouldn't shoot anyone without a damned good reason, but it made a credible threat to an outsider.

She could hear combat ongoing in the other room and saw the back of Jake's head as he wrestled with someone.

Hollyanne wasn't sure what she could do to help.

THIRTY-SEVEN

JAKE HAD TANGLED NATHANIEL CLOSE, four snakes writhing in a ball trying to gain a superior position. Sharks sniffing for blood.

Nathaniel had spent his time in prison practicing his forms, that much was certain. He was at least as good as Jake was.

That was bad.

He was holding the man even right now, but that was about it.

"Why?" Nathaniel hissed at him.

They weren't close enough to exchange headbutts, but only because both of them were leaning back enough to be safe from a stinger to the nose.

"You could have stayed in prison," Jake growled back, still maneuvering.

Each hand that slipped found a new grip, but the arm gripped slipped in turn and broke.

"Never," Nathaniel snarled. "I will beat you yet."

The man had a surge of mad strength now that turned them sideways in the room. Jake found himself pressed against the edge of the desk and losing his leverage slowly.

Inexorably.

He struggled anyway.

"You created Pacific Force," Jake reminded him, fighting things back to a standstill. "Without you aiming to be a supervillain, we'd have never had to band together to stop you."

Jake was rewarded by a hiss of pure anger from the man.

More wrestling. More blows that traveled no more than an inch before being tangled or deflected. But Jake got back a little space.

"Now that you're back, we're back," Jake continued. "The world isn't safe because of people like you, but we're not corrupt."

"Everyone's corrupt," Nathaniel's voice rose now. "I couldn't exist if there were honest governments, or even honest men running them. You'll never stop that."

"Maybe," Jake shrugged as much as he could. Nathaniel would feel it through their struggle. "But you've already lost because I have everyone with me tonight. And Grant is bringing the government folks. Now would be a good time to surrender."

"I will never surrender," Nathaniel howled. "You will never beat me."

"Good," Hollyanne's voice suddenly broke in. "I was hoping for a repeat engagement."

Jake felt Nathaniel glance over and noted the shadow in the door. Short. Smelled like lilacs. Jake was pretty sure none of Nathaniel's men wore that particular scent.

"Shit," Nathaniel grunted.

His struggles continued, but Jake could feel defeat seeping into the man.

"You want to die right here, or go back to prison?" Jake asked. "Your choice."

It was only partially a threat. The world might be better off without Nathaniel Hoestler's genius stirring things up on the wrong side of the law. The British government wouldn't be feeling particularly benevolent, even if nobody was hurt by that bomb.

Those scars went deep, however self-inflicted they were.

"You win," Nathaniel said, relaxing his grip and shifting his feet. "For now."

"For now," Jake agreed.

He'd known the man since they were thirteen. Recruited him and Spencer at the same time into the little computer club that had made most of them rich. Nathaniel Hoestler would have been, as well, but he'd struck out on his own after an angry confrontation, and then been bitten in the ass when Jake sold his little company at the peak of the dot-com market valuations.

Six months later, when Nathaniel had been prepared, there was no money left for him to strike back.

The littlest things that can change the course of human history.

Nathaniel let go and stepped back. He stared at Hollyanne for a long moment and then pulled his chair and sat.

"If I thought it would do any good, I'd show you some of the stuff I was planning to steal tonight," he said in a dejected, almost-defeated tone. But only almost. "The Intelligence Services maintain their own files on misconduct and blackmail. Not that they use them but so that they can understand when they need to quietly whisper in someone's ear about retirements."

"And you'd have gotten back in the game with that power," Jake said, standing just out of reach of a hand or foot, but he didn't think Nathaniel was a risk now.

Pacific Force stood between him and freedom.

"I would have," Nathaniel agreed. "Most of these people should be arrested and thrown out of office, but they all have a vested interest in keeping it secret, so nobody ever does anything about it, except for an occasional reporter getting a tip and striking hard with it. But even those are calculated to only damage certain people. The system remains."

"Perhaps, but you are going about cleaning it up the wrong way," Jake said. "Let's go tie you up with the others. Company is about twenty minutes behind us."

"How the hell did you get here so quickly?" Nathaniel asked as he rose and started slowly forward.

"Grant was the one that found your bombmaker," Jake said as they emerged into the hallway, Hollyanne leading the man into the other room past Tommy's unconscious form.

"But nobody could have figured this out," Nathaniel continued. "And where were you?"

"We came into Manchester at the same time Grant did." Jake smiled. "Had to keep you guessing. From there, Rik lined us up for a night jump to skydive in on the target once it had been identified."

"Night jump?" Nathaniel asked, incredulous. "Are you insane?"

Jake just smiled at the man.

"Wrists," he said.

Nathaniel held his out and Jake took a set of ties from Hollyanne's hands and closed them. He relieved Nathaniel of everything in his pockets as Hollyanne dragged Tommy in and did the same to the other two men.

"When do we get let out?" one of the two men on the couch asked now.

"When the British government gets here and takes charge," Jake said.

"British government?" the man flinched in surprise. "Then who the hell are you people?"

"We're Pacific Force," Jake smiled at the man.

191

EPILOGUE

JAKE WAS in his kitchen with the team. Thursday morning had dawned and faded. Mrs. Johnson had made everyone breakfast and then gone back to mixing in the cottage, leaving the five of them alone in the main house. Grant and Spencer were on his right with Hollyanne and Rik on his left.

Jake sipped at his espresso and thought dark and sour thoughts.

"Hey, dude, cheer up," Rik said, looking in Jake's direction. "We pulled it off and got everyone home safely."

Jake stirred, but Hollyanne spoke.

"Nathaniel made some ugly accusations there at the end," Hollyanne replied. "Most of them were probably true, too."

"You think the British government is that bent?" Grant spoke up.

"If Nathaniel didn't, he would have never tried that mission," Spencer replied. "That much risk. That much bribe money. There had to be a reward commensurate with it. He was convinced that the information he would have stolen would have set him up."

"But he's gone for good this time, right?" Grant asked.

"He is," Jake agreed. "Okay, I have a question for all of you now."

Before he could get any farther, his cell phone rang.

Spencer had programmed all of their phones to go straight to voicemail if the number wasn't programmed in, although Jake had never asked how. You weren't supposed to be able to do that without seriously jailbreaking it first. And updates were supposed to override those sorts of things.

They had a rule about phones at the breakfast table, but again, it rang, so Jake reached out a hand and flipped it over to see who was wanting his attention this morning.

Sir William calling…

Jake considered putting it on speaker but put it to his ear instead.

"Good morning, sir," he answered. "How may we be of service today?"

"I thought you should be among the first to know," Sir William replied in his quiet, posh tones. "Roughly three hours ago, the vehicle transporting your friend Nathaniel Hoestler was reported missing. Obviously, investigations are on-going, and I am assured by relevant contacts that your group has returned to Seattle for the time being."

"That's correct, Sir William," Jake replied. "We flew out Wednesday afternoon once everything in London was resolved. Is there anything we can do?"

"At this point, we'll either have him in hand again within a few hours, or—and this is the more likely scenario, I'm afraid—he will have slipped entirely away, and we'll have to start the investigation from scratch."

"Who else disappeared?" Jake asked.

"What makes you think others did?" Sir William asked, a bit astonished.

"That tells me if this was a random fluke," Jake said. "A door left open sort of thing versus a contingency he had already put in place."

"Ah, I see," the man said. "Your pardon."

Jake heard a hand muffling the handset at the other end, so he looked at everyone.

"Someone walked away from his chain gang," Jake told the others quietly.

The scowls were rather harsh, but it was early, and everyone had just had a wonderful breakfast that was digesting.

"Jake? I'm given to understand that Thomas Wilcox remains yet in custody," Sir William came back a moment later. "However, the other fellow you captured, Sokoro Otieno, has disappeared. That tall, Kenyan chap. As for the rest, I would like to set up a call for Saturday. Just after midday your time would be late in my afternoon, and I can update you then."

"I look forward to it, Sir William," Jake said. "Thank you."

The man hung up quickly, and Jake looked at the others.

"Nathaniel and Lucky were being transported when their vehicle just disappeared," he said simply. "Tommy's still in jail, at least for now."

"What does he think we can do from here?" Hollyanne asked abruptly.

"Nothing," Jake replied. "He wants to call me in about fifty-two hours and let me know if Nathaniel indeed got away, but I don't really have my doubts."

"Because Lucky went with him?" Spencer asked.

"He is called Lucky for a reason," Jake reminded them.

"So now what?" Grant asked.

"So now, we need to talk," Jake said, inwardly cringing

at the choice of words but understanding that there was no easy way to say it. "Two years ago, we put that man in prison for what should have been twenty years and then Pacific Force retired as a group."

"You never stopped working," Hollyanne pointed out as Rik nodded.

"Correct." Jake nodded compactly. "Not that long ago, I helped our old friend Perkins bust a smuggling ring here in Seattle, but that's me. The rest of you have your own lives."

"But Nathaniel's back," Hollyanne stated.

"Ten minutes ago, I was all set to say thanks to the four of you for helping me out one last time," Jake said. "But now…"

"About that," Rik, of all people, spoke up. "I kinda enjoyed myself more than I expected. I realized that I'd been coasting a lot for the last couple of years. Pacific Force made me stretch muscles that were starting to get a little slack and lazy."

Jake turned to the boys on his right, facing inward towards the wall.

"Spencer?" Jake asked.

"I suppose this is where I admit I might have been working as a bit more of an undercover, muck-raking reporter than I might have mentioned to the rest of you," he said with an evasive smile. "Nothing as big as Jake, but also not retired. However, doing it with the team is always more rewarding."

"Grant?" Jake asked next, smiling at Spencer.

"I've been in Canada lately," he said, also a little evasive.

"You running a con on the government or a woman?" Rik asked with a rude smile.

Grant flinched and grimaced.

"Maybe a little of both?" he replied after a moment.

"Oh?"

"She wants me to settle down and become something of a trophy husband," Grant said. "You know, cocktail parties, opera, tuxedos, power lunches, afternoon tennis. Not a euphemism."

"Not a euphemism," Jake repeated with a laugh. "But you're bored, aren't you?"

"Out of my freaking mind," Grant replied. "I've almost been reduced to running cons on the ladies at the market, just to keep busy."

"I take it you don't have to rush right back off?" Jake asked.

"I'm sure you need me for some secret project, and I'll only be able to slip into Canada for a day or a long weekend at a time."

"You will break up with her, then," Rik snapped in an ugly tone suggesting way more than Jake was able to place. "Right now."

"Yes, ma'am," Grant replied, thoroughly chastened.

Jake drew a breath as every head turned to the last person at the table.

Hollyanne had been silent. Contemplative.

Anybody else, and Jake would have said uncertain, but he knew her better than just about anyone. If they'd both been a little different, they'd have probably been celebrating a twentieth wedding anniversary soon, instead of just an upcoming twentieth high school reunion, but they'd never quite clicked that way, and neither had wanted to tear apart what they had by forcing it.

Pacific Force had always been more important, and then she'd disappeared for much of the last two years, only popping up on his radar intermittently.

"Hollyanne?" Jake asked. "What do you think?"

"I think we were a force for good, once," she said with a stern face.

"Once?" Jake countered.

"We retired." She turned to face him, as though they were alone in the room. "Went our separate ways. Maybe needed to find ourselves, or at least our purpose."

Jake didn't figure she was talking about anyone but herself, but also didn't feel like pointing that out. Hollyanne Kadjar had always been the philosopher of the group. The deep thinker exploring the ethics and morality of the thing, even as she was the tank who waded into combat with people like Mikhail or Lucky.

"And now?" Jake prodded her when she fell silent.

The others were silent. Possibly not even breathing right now.

"And now, Nathaniel is a threat again," she finally admitted. "Like you, I had thought we'd all separate now and vanish again, but he's out there."

"If Pacific Force wasn't revived, I doubt Nathaniel would come after any of us individually," Jake offered. "Those old rules were always honored. He chose to surrender at the end, when one of us might have killed him. I suppose he knew he had one last surprise for us but we found the narrow boat and caught those folks as well. Most of his organization is gone now, except for Lucky and whoever he can recruit now."

"But that's just it," she said in a voice verging on anguish. "He will rebuild. He's that good. You've said that nobody but Pacific Force can stop the man. I have no doubt that you're right."

"And?" Jake asked.

"And I'm not sure what's next," she replied.

"What do you want, Hollyanne?" Jake asked her. "What would bring joy and peace to the warrior monk?"

"I wanted him done," Hollyanne said. "I almost did that two years ago, but we captured him instead. And now he's escaped us again."

She fell silent, dark eyes staring at him.

Jake waited.

"I don't know what I want," she finally admitted.

Jake wasn't surprised. He'd known that about her for years. The only astonishment on his part was that she had maybe finally realized it herself.

"I'd like your help," Jake said, leaving the shape of the commitment open for interpretation, unwilling to push just yet.

She'd been his best friend for more twenty years, even occasional lovers like Rik, but nothing more and he had no claim on her now.

"Will it be enough?" she asked, and Jake saw the heart of her conundrum.

Would it be enough? Would it ever be enough? Could they say for certain that they had made the world a better place, short of someone finally killing Nathaniel?

But he also understood the answer that she needed in order to make her way past the trap she'd talked herself into. The philosophical quagmire of thought disrupting deeds.

"We will leave the world a better place than we found it," Jake said. "That will be enough."

She drew a breath to argue with him, but they'd had this discussion so many times that he could probably recite the words as fast as she would say them. After a moment, she smiled crookedly, as if she recognized that.

Instead, Hollyanne lifted her coffee mug in a toast.

"To Pacific Force," she offered.

"Pacific Force," the others responded and everyone drank.

Jake smiled. He'd been carrying the load alone for the last two years, but now he would have help.

Because Pacific Force had returned.

READ MORE

To read more of my fiction, sign up for my newsletter. You'll also get a free book!

http://www.blazeward.com/newsletter/

ABOUT THE AUTHOR

Blaze Ward is a prolific Indie writer and publisher who works mostly in Science Fiction and Light Thriller, with occasional forays into lots of other genres like superheroic fantasy.

You can find more of his titles at www.blazeward.com/books, www.KnottedRoadPress.com and wherever else you buy your books.

He also edits Boundary Shock Quarterly, an SF magazine he founded in 2018, and Thrill Ride Magazine.

ABOUT KNOTTED ROAD PRESS

Knotted Road Press publishes dynamic fiction set in exotic locations. Our authors cover a wide range of genres including science fiction, fantasy, mystery, literary, and poetry. We also have unique non-fiction voices in genres such as autobiography, business, cookbooks, and how-tos. We offer both DRM-free ebooks and print books for a global readership.

www.KnottedRoadPress.com

www.ingramcontent.com/pod-product-compliance
Lightning Source LLC
Chambersburg PA
CBHW070536100726
47907CB00004B/1145